RAMBLINGS

Charlie James Brown

Fulton Books, Inc.
Meadville, PA

First originally published by Fulton Books 2017

ISBN 978-1-63338-708-9 (Paperback)
ISBN 978-1-63338-600-6 (Hard Cover)
ISBN 978-1-63338-601-3 (Digital)

Printed in the United States of America

December 17, 2016

This book is dedicated in loving memory to
Wilhelmina Elizabeth Whitenack, who was called
home on January 15, 1967.
My beloved Aunt Betty, mother, teacher, protector,
and angel for the true innocents entrusted to her care.

—*Charlie James Brown*

October 4, 2017

Dear Joseph & Margaret,

Nothing lasts forever
except forever.

Consider today a gift,
that is why it's called
'the present'.

Pax Vobiscum,
Charlie James Brown

CONTENTS

INTRODUCTION

As you can see, I am not a prolific writer. My very first poem, "Spare Me This Sight," was written at the age of fourteen in 1961, inspired by the Civil War Centennial.

"Ode to South Vietnam," written in 2010, was inspired by a WWII poem, "Letter to Saint Peter" by Elma Dean, written approximately in 1943. I served in the US Navy from 1964 to 1968 as a hospital corpsman assigned with the USMC in the First Corps zone of South Vietnam from 1965 to 1967.

A couple of my earliest poems were written at the age of fourteen and fifteen, and these I have parenthesized as kids' stuff. After my entry into the military and adult working career, I did, to the best of my knowledge, very little of what I refer to as painting pictures with words, my synonym for writing. It was only after my retirement in 2005 that I found the time and opportunity to reflect back upon my life from a higher vantage point with life experience and all that goes with it that, as most of my senior readers will agree, change our perceptions and priorities immensely.

To any folks out there that might consider purchasing *Ramblings*, I want to say that I have tried as much as I can to dive into the deepest depths, especially in my poems. I have rewritten some a dozen times or more to question and explore the remotest boundaries of my soul and discern, examine, and put into words whatever I've found there. My ultimate goal is to share with my readers the meticulously dissected essence of perceptions as revealed to me by my senses when probed so deeply. Be it good, bad, soothing, or racked with pain. My hope would be for perhaps a pearl or two to be found by them as they follow this rambling odyssey to its last page.

Most sincerely,

Charlie James Brown

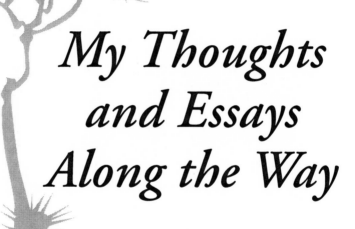

My Thoughts
and Essays
Along the Way

RAMBLING WITH THE RAMBLER

Rambling as defined in the Random House Dictionary of the English Language, 1981 unabridged edition, page 1189 is as follows:

a)   Aimlessly wandering
b)   Taking an irregular course, straggling
c)   Spread out irregularly in various directions
d)   Straying from one subject to another

My personal opinion of advice and philosophy is akin to mud.

With this in mind, come with me on this ramble. If, perchance, you find anything of interest, pick up a handful and test it by throwing it against the barn house wall. If any of it sticks, keep it; otherwise, keep walking.

Remembering, of course, when you cry, you cry alone.

When you laugh, the whole world laughs with you.

Old Polish proverb: "Too soon we get old, too late we get smart."

I want it all! Food, water, and love.

Eureka! I was born to be a new nuance to the comment "ill conceived." A new connotation that explains all!

Stick with me, and you'll be wearing diamonds as big as horse turds!

Peggy Lee's song said it eloquently: "Is that all there is?"

The most precious gift we can give to someone is our time.

Expect to be challenged at least once a day, if not more.

No one can walk the halls of my thoughts or open the doors of my past unless I give them the key.

Be thankful for the few joys and life lived when compared to that of others you have met along the way.

Never compare yourself to others, for there will always be those greater and lesser than yourself.

Who says the CREATOR has no sense of humor? When at last you can fit together what pieces of life there are, it's time to go!

It's okay not to feel okay every day.

The graveyards are filled with unfulfilled potential.

Was he a credit to his gender?

I was told I was a latex failure. Love child never meant to be.

Born to die. What else?

Awaken! The show must go on. Dance to the music!

The awesome tenacity of the human mind overshadows those found in nature in that we are aware of our inevitable end to the journey here.

Having your eyes open every morning is a good indicator.

Strive to be comfortable in your own skin.

The only constant thing in life is change.

The incomprehensible sight of the carnage, high-velocity metal can inflict upon the human anatomy of young men serving their country. Following out orders is something I wish for all who call others to war to experience!

Life has taught me that only the thinnest of lines separate ambition from greed.

Waylon Jennings, Johnny Cash, George Jones, Merle Haggard, and Willie Nelson. Who's going to fill their shoes? Answer: Ain't nobody gonna ever fill their shoes! It can never be done again. The mold is broken. The caliber of our singing poet laureates will never rise to this level again no matter how many more millenniums this Earth survives.

Want justice? Go to a whorehouse. Want to get screwed? Go to court.

Alone we come into this world, and alone we leave it, as it should be.

How can they know me? I hardly know myself, with so many pieces of my life's puzzle missing.

Life is not worth living if you do not have beliefs, values, or dreams that are so important to your existence you would not hesitate to die for them.

I am. I did exist.

The only place you will ever find sympathy is in the dictionary, between *shit* and *syphilis.*

I have found the heightened emotions of digging up the past to be a great laxative, if good for nothing else.

Quote from Eleanor Roosevelt: "Yesterday is history, tomorrow is a mystery, and today is a gift; that's why they call it the present."

I must add this most meaningful quote from the great Lebanese American poet and writer Kahlil Gibran: "You talk when you cease to be at peace with your thoughts; and when you can no longer dwell in the solitude of your heart you live in your lips, and sound is a diversion and a pastime. And in much of your talking, thinking is half murdered. For thought is a bird of space, that in a cage of words may indeed unfold its wings but cannot fly."

Pragmatism begins with knowing for a fact that each day your eyes open will not always be warm and fuzzy. Being pragmatic is knowing it is the rare exception and not the rule. Knowing this makes the exception even more rewarding, so try to prolong and savor each precious moment when and if it does occur.

Enough! Hope some, if any, sticks for you.

CAN YOU IMAGINE?

December 5, 2016

A world without the complete repertoire of melodic perfection as songbirds court their mates? The absence of an orchestrated symphony between crickets, cicadas, and frogs expressing their joy of being alive in nocturnal unison, building to an anticipated crescendo as the first rays of a new dawn begin to pierce the absence of light?

The loss of auditory perception is never fully appreciated until its dome of buffered silence incrementally envelopes its unfortunate recipient. It has no outward appearances of traumatic amputations lost in war or the panic attacks of minds revisiting those horrors again and again.

But in reality, it is a most stealthful thief. Exiling one to an island where fellow victims colonize in an attempt to commiserate their losses. Victims robbed of confidence and the ability to fully communicate with their peers. These social voids are quickly filled with feelings of self-loathing, degradation, anger, and frustration.

But this saga has a dramatic reversal of fortunes brought on by the empathy, dedication, and technology utilized by the knights and princesses of the VAMC Decatur, Georgia, audiology clinic! They ride forth every day to slay the dragon of deafness and build a bridge to the island, allowing its refugees to once again return to society. May they all now be recognized for restoring us to the world of sound and communication, so often taken lightly for granted by those not afflicted, be it between mice or men!

YES OR NO?

2016

Dare I think or dream of an awareness beyond the realm of this one that has consumed my every conscious moment?

A place or dimension so unknown it defies logic as we perceive it. The thought of its existence is incomprehensible to the limits of mere mortals.

Be it utopia, Shangri-La, Valhalla, nirvana, paradise, the happy hunting ground, somewhere over the rainbow, a better place, heaven, or hell.

A one-way journey inevitable to all, where none return to tell a word. Is it a reality or merely absurd?

THE REAPER

January 17, 2016

It is good the young have no superficial realization of the fragility, duration, and comparative rapid passage of this life. Especially when the perception of it becomes acutely apparent as we near its end. For if they do, we with seniority, nearing the end of our journeys, can never enjoy and witness the rhythm of their dance.

I saw him again today. Through my peripheral vision I caught momentarily a glimpse of the darkness of the cape as he quickly recoiled from his observation site. He shadows me, for that is his assignment.

I am on the list, as are we all, the chronology of course unknown. But its culmination is assuredly inevitable. I may be of special interest as I have escaped his grasp upon a few occasions in years past.

Sadly, I know that I have not made the most of these precious years gifted. Perhaps that introspective fact will spur me on with a renewal of purpose while I stand here within the bottom of life's hourglass. Perched now am I on a mountain of sand, feeling small grains from above just frugally dusting from what was in times past a robust storm of sand.

IN THE PALM OF MY HAND

January 2016

I held the small feathered body in the palm of my hand. Still conscious, it was obvious he was seriously stunned. My initial observation was drawn to the alignment of symmetrical design highlighted with various colors of plumage, a masterpiece born of some higher power. As I gently stroked his head, his open but dazed eyes focused directly into mine.

I saw no blood or evidence of fracture from his full flight collision with the windowpane. Slowly the curled toes of both feet twitched then stretched out to gain a foothold in my palm as he stood up, still his eyes wavering not from mine.

I continued to slowly stroke a larger area, now including neck and back. I wanted to convey the message that was impossible to semantically verbalize. My intention was to speak through reassuring tactile movements that no harm or threat would dissipate these fleeting magical moments.

It appeared he was regaining full alertness, the once dull eyes now clear and bright, as if he could search with penetrating gaze and know the secrets of my soul. I wanted so much to slow life's clock, to prolong these mystical seconds in time when avian and human stood as equals on this plane of emotion. An epic truce of commonality, a bonding of nature and man.

He may have blinked once, possibly twice, as if acknowledging the epiphany of it all. Every beginning has an end, and with an abrupt flutter of wings, he flew to the nearest tree. We could still see each other in the distance now. Perhaps we will both occasionally reflect on this little gemstone of time stored in the treasure chest of life's memories before we can both fly away on our inevitable adventure to come.

FOR PANCHITA

December 30, 2015

Singer Peggy Lee said, "Is that all there is?" in her song of that title. Thinking along that trend of thought, I say…

Fan the smoldering embers of memories lost to see again the cost of so many good souls now departed. In the rekindled flame he now remembers their peals of laughter from afar, the uniqueness of each one, so filled with youth and yet untainted. In that time of here and now, with never a thought of tomorrows.

Pearls of life, love, and the joys of living. Strong and without fear, bodies of beauty and imaginations to touch the stars. We danced the dance. In those hours and days, a flame's flicker of time.

All of us now so grateful we were given that chance.

For my mother-in-law, Francisca Malvido de Valle, who passed today at the age of ninety-one on a new adventure.

LAST VOYAGE TO CAMELOT

August 30, 2014

Adrift on the ocean in the midst of raging storms, this once majestic ship of state finds itself in dire peril. It's captain, for all practical purposes, is absent. Helmsmen, mates, and navigator cringing in the panic of novices on their first voyage in rough seas. The rudder now gone, with winds pushing the hull to the rocks and shoals of our enemies, waiting with bated anticipation for our imminent destruction. Even the once faithful crew has sold their souls to the devil. Betrayed have they, the very basics of the enlistment tenets they swore to defend.

Crumpled charts now adrift with the bloated bodies and parts mixed with the flotsam and jetsam of what was once the grandest lady to ever sail the seas. Its running lights so powerful as to pierce the darkness of worldly despair and bring a spark of hope to the oppressed everywhere. Symbol of salvation, her mere presence on the horizon struck fear into the heart of evil and inspiration to the huddled masses yearning to be free.

Now gone forever, shattered wreckage sunken fathoms beneath the briny foam. The calming water smooth as glass rippled only by the sharks as they rise to feed.

OPEN LETTER TO AMERICAN CITIZENS

July 2014

In the first place, the federal government has no business being in the medical business, with the exception of the Veterans Administration or Medicare. This huge bureaucracy continues to encroach yearly into our private lives and in many more places a democratic republic has no right interfering in. The rules of the peoples' government are guaranteed in the Constitution and Bill of Rights our Founding Fathers wrote down to sustain and protect "We, the people."

In my sixty-seven years since being born in the U.S.A., I have seen our freedoms and constitutional rights be progressively eroded by the shadow of big government casting its shroud of tyranny over this vast nation from coast to coast. Believe me when I say to you, the younger generations born after me, that you have no idea of the scope of negative change that has evolved in the above noted time frame.

I look around in these present day times and see the police state continue its erosion in what was once called the land of the free and the home of the brave. At times I really think I am living in some repressive third world country! The appalling lack of leadership in our presidents, Obama being the latest and worst I have ever seen, is shameful, to say the least! Forgoing monitoring oversight or term limits as we vote into offices of responsibility divisive and corruption-prone representatives is a psychotic way to have a democratic government run!

We, the people, as a nation are supposed to control the tenure of power through the vote of the majority of us when we grant this sacred trust to send these privileged, elected officials to Washington, DC. They have the duty to be the watchdogs of our tax dollars and to be stewards of the protection of the rights guaranteed to us in this nation. The Constitution and its amenities spell this out empathically; we are not deaf, blind, or dumb, as some of you may think. Our most glaring apathy is in not voting. Perhaps you think your vote "does not count," but I say to you most unequivocally that IT DOES! That right to vote has been consecrated in the supreme sacrifice of men and women who have given up their lives at the altar of war to ensure that privilege continues, and no power on earth can change that. To NOT VOTE is a most disgraceful insult and dishonor to the memory of those brave, patriotic souls, past and present.

The skillful but corruptive, manipulative practices of many, but not the majority, of the presently seated elected officials have been used against us to their advantage for the profit and agendas of outside forces and special interest groups. FORGET NOT, MY FELLOW CITIZENS, that the most egregious forms of gerrymandering tactics employed by the jaded career politicians are meant to remove us from the equation our Founding Fathers had envisioned and put authority and power in the hands of a few!

Big government has placed us under their thumbs and dictated to the masses during recent decades past. It will most definitively take undivided attention and a strong will to see us right through these wrongs. WE MUST ALL UNITE! We must stop the bickering and backstabbing for personal gain or stupid prejudices and stereotypes. Nothing gives these corrupt incumbents more pleasure and security than to see us divided and fighting among ourselves. When will we ever learn? When will we stop fighting over cultures, religions, lifestyles, and skin colors? When will the time for the words "Power to the people" take on the strength and unity it was meant to convey when first spoken? This journey at this time of chaos will be long; it will hurt, some of us will not live to see the goal attained, but it must begin NOW! This enormous ship of state will take time to respond to new helmsmen and helmswomen dedicated to see it change direction and return to the course that four decades of "political pirates" have circumvented us as a nation from. Remember always that our strength comes from our diversity and determination to see the job done regardless of cost, pain, imprisonment, or death. Alone we are lost. All the blood ever shed on the battlefield throughout the ages was red—remember that!

If you, young folks out there, are seriously ready for a change, it will be your destiny to shoulder the majority of the load to save your country domestically from within. Throw away the video games and grab up the voter registration cards; time is of the essence! Spread the word through the social media you are so adept at. The American Spring is getting fired up! The people will take no more abuse! We are coming, November 2014. Register to vote and then make damn sure you do it! Bring into the Senate, Congress, and executive and judicial branches young men and women with fresh ideas and solutions to these old problems. Force term limits or a mandatory retirement age on all who serve. Repeal lifetime appointments, especially in the judiciary; it is absolute disaster to allow this practice to continue.

Last of all, I say to anyone now "serving" the people of these United States of America, if you are over the age of seventy years old, resign or retire honorably. GO HOME! You old fools, your time has come and gone! Get off the stage! You are stinking the place up! If you haven't fixed it by now, you certainly won't in the time left to you. Our Founding Fathers NEVER meant for you to make a lifetime career of politics. Stand aside! The American Spring is fueling up and getting ready to swiftly roll down the tracks at the dawn of a new day for this beleaguered nation! A truly legitimate new day, not campaign bullshit! If you stand in its way, you do so at your own peril!

OUR COUNTRY IN TURMOIL

June 14, 2014

To whom it may concern:

Flip-flopping Eric Cantor, majority House leader, is the first of many on both sides of the aisle that will fall in November. The so-called establishment in Washington, DC, apparently still does not have their finger on us, the electorate's pulse.

Yes, we, the people, are, at long last, sick and tired of Washington's lack of response and redundant rhetoric that accompanies their lack of ACTION on any or all illegal actions and irresponsibility being perpetrated on them by the present administration and its dupes.

A government, at all levels, that has failed the people miserably. It has lost all creditability as it has distanced itself from the plight of the people. The majority, not all, are narcissistic, patronizing old farts that think of themselves as beyond the laws they dictate to we the people, both ethically and in the spirit of the law. Many have spent decades feeding at the public trough, assuming in their egotistical self-perception that term limits on the FEDERAL LEVEL will never happen. Wrong! Everyone can and will be replaced. We must bring in young blood with new ideas to help solve the same old problems that have plagued this country for at least fifty years now. When will they ever learn from the history of their recent past?

To think we drug test new hires for a ten-dollar-an-hour-job and add psychological testing profiles to that for safety and first responders yet allow someone to assume the most powerful position in the land, ad hoc, is ludicrous! The corruption from within, at all levels, rivals that of Athens and Rome. We may even be at that point of no return. The inmates run this asylum. Apathy is rampant.

As a nation of sheep spoken about in a book of the past entitled *1984*, we have now reached critical mass. In my lifetime I saw the best of this country post-WWII and the fifties. The distorted, convoluted nation that we still call the *United* States is anything but that now. Sadly, the light that once shined as the beacon of hope for the world has now faded from the horizon. We are mocked worldwide and taken advantage of by the world that can predict our every move, with our porous borders never stemming the tide. They steal our intellectual treasures and secrets and spill the lifeblood of our young men, and now young women, on wars we should never have been involved in, from Vietnam to the present point in time. I speak from personal experience of the fiasco of Republic of South Vietnam (1964–1968), where 58,237 heroes fell in a civil war we had no business being in, now our trading partner! Once again, I cry out for my brothers that sacrificed their lives and now fill the graveyards with their unfilled potential. I have spoken to deaf ears; I have screamed out loud to the heavens in the worst of storms, "OH GOD, when will THEY ever learn?"

I have concluded, NEVER. As long as it is not their sons and daughters put in harm's way for no logical reason, when you boil it down to the bare bones.

This present administration is a travesty from the top of Obama's head to the tip of his toes, yet you all that were sent to the hill to protect our backs have done nothing, except for the far too few valiant souls who are receiving this letter. The emperor and the hacks surrounding him have no clothes! To this very day they have yet to realize this fact as they are still in campaign mode six and a half devastating years later!

Now is the last time to call all good men and women to come to the aid of their country before it slips beneath the waves of history.

THE NEW ERA DAWNS

May 29, 2014

The dawn of a new era in our history lies on the horizon for our beleaguered nation.

Imagine and dream of what could be accomplished if only we find the willpower once more to lift ourselves from the ashes of recent years. Renew our hope in the light of democracy dimmed but not yet extinguished. We must use the privilege to vote responsibly in much greater numbers, letting not a few dictate to the masses. Take time to verify the histories of candidates, their politics and morals. We must send the best and brightest to Washington, DC, with fresh, new approaches to the same old problems that have plagued us for decades.

United once more, we will emerge with the strength forged in the fires of recent diversity and mistrust. Temper a bond of cooperation and integrity nationwide. Celebrate and embrace a new epiphany of what the most multicultural country to ever exist on the face of this Earth can achieve when acting in unison!

With the rebirth of a new administration of leadership that is dedicated to the tenets our Founding Fathers laid out for us in the Constitution and Bill of Rights. Needed is a responsive government that truly has its finger on the pulse of all its citizens and acts in accordance with honesty, determination, and purpose. Doing the right thing for the good of the majority and the best interests of the country must always be its number-one priority regardless of political ideology. We, the people, will no longer accept anything less, so help us GOD!

ALPHABET OF LIFE

2014

Memories and thoughts prevail as they steadfastly forge their way through every letter of the alphabet of life.

In times of insult, rage, anger, or heartfelt resentment, maintain the discipline to narrow your focus only on the offending individual.

Block the reactionary urge to encompass a culture, religion, skin color, political view, or even present day divisiveness.

Focus as hard as it may be on what was said or done to ignite the fire he or she has brought to you.

Paint with the fine brush of an artist and do not sweep with the broom of the streets.

SUN RISES OR SUN SETS

2013

For many, seeing the sun rise symbolizes eternal birth or a new cycle of life. For other observers, it might arise with thorns of its own. I find that unless it is viewed through an opaque lens, filters, or the shading provided by a forest of ancient coastal redwood trees, it presents subliminal difficulties of perception.

At this stage of life, I prefer the setting sundown as it descends on far horizons with incremental speed. It placidly prods the subconscious to release recollections hidden within the extreme boundaries of its being. Perhaps they were only preserved for hallowed moments like this. The briefest synopsis of life, with no time to dwell in meticulous detail. It can be viewed straight on with all shades up and barriers and drawbridges down. Reflections of the past tease fleetingly by, reducing one to the flotsam, at the mercy of life's currents, floating with surrender. I like sunsets.

CHANGING OF THE GUARD

July 2013

Amazing statistic revealed by demographers last week. For the first time since the founding of this country, the Caucasian death rate exceeded the Caucasian birth rate.

Our strength has always been in our diversity, but I wonder why 72 percent of black babies are born to single-parent homes. Showing a black drug dealer's face on television laughing about being sire to twenty-two babies with fourteen different women and also bragging about his nonpayment of child support makes me wonder what agenda the media is trying to portray with this negative example.

Is the ability to plant a seed valued more today than the responsible farmer who labors hard to bring his crop to maturity? Is this just presented to us as someone's jaded idea of "entertainment"? Surely, their thought was not to present him as a role model, or was it? Why even exhibit this indignity before the public eye? All you beautiful young and older women know that it takes two to tango. Are you totally devoid of parental responsibility and self-esteem? Why would you not want the best advantages possible for yourselves and the children you bring into this competitive world? The world is progressively changing into a place where only those who are willing to focus on goals and be prepared to meet the challenges, hard work, and determination that this entails will succeed. Two people bonding to achieve success have the advantage over just one. You can do better when you think ahead about the consequences of your actions today in relation to the priority you place on your future as a couple. You all can try harder, search longer, and have faith in yourselves, a higher power, or both, if so inclined.

For my Latino family, I will refer you to the above and tell you that the way to seek a goal does not always justify the ends. "Anchor babies"?

Echar en cara a uno su negligencia, hacerle sonrojar por su descuido! It is much less difficult in the long journey of life to start off by doing things in the right way. You may not like the laws, but I say to you, it will save you much pain, suffering, and lifetime wasted to accept them than to lose all when you choose to oppose them. The odds, like in Las Vegas, are against you. Once that line is crossed in a few seconds of mindless emotions, it can never be reversed.

It is so shameful and disgusting to see 2.3 million young men and women locked away in prisons in this country, with their entire lives before them now hopelessly ruined! More than any other country's percentage of population are incarcerated here than any other place in the entire world.

I say these things because I care for you and my country. I, like so many others, have been to war for this land of ours. The real heroes of which have never returned alive. I tell you this because based on the facts I mentioned in my opening, both my black and brown brothers and sisters will inherit this nation based on figures of birth rate that show you all as being the majority of our population by 2050, if not sooner. With that majority comes responsibility. We need moral leaders with foresight and conviction, better role models for the children, and for those who do achieve the pinnacle, I say to you, DO NOT forget your roots and the struggle—pay some back. If ever we are to succeed, we must stop the constant infighting agitated by a few for reasons of selfish agendas or profit. Make no mistake of that, my brothers and sisters! The worst nightmare of the elitist 5 percent is to see the working class of this country stop fighting among themselves and UNITE! Believe me, seeing the power of the people united as one would turn them to pillars of salt before they could place one foot in front of the other.

Please give my words some thought; it is in your hands now, and I will be long gone, for better or worse. It is up to the young citizens of today to take the reins of power.

Last of all, I wish to say to all fools and bigots living among us in our diverse cultures, religions, politics, skin colors, and the like that your days are numbered. Humanity's goodness will eventually be triumphant. The seeds of evil you are sowing will never come to harvest because we are many and you are few. I've not always walked the straight and narrow during my journey, but at this time of life in my fading years, I no longer see differences, but similarities. I only see their eyes, the windows of the soul, from my present vantage point. I respect and treat well those who share likewise with me. Along with life and the human dignity given by the Creator to all is our uniqueness in the family of human beings. It is here we share the predominant common denominator. Nothing within the realm of this earth can separate us from our birthright unless we comply or submit to it. Throughout the ages, in all the futile and wasteful wars and the loss of the intangible spark of countless lives on the battlefields of history, the blood spilled has always been red.

4 ON 1: T + H + F + C

2010

Just a Thought
In the early mists of fog-clouded mornings do my thoughts take liberties and yearn to escape these earthly bonds and soar as if on the majestic wings of eagles, angels, and unicorns to distant realms where time matters not and tranquility reigns supreme in the universe of dreams undreamt.

Hope
I could hope for change. Hope that would clear the board of all vestiges of evil and inhumanity to man perpetrated by man. I could hope for the world of "somewhere over the rainbow," of nature and mankind in a true balance of empathy, like dreamers of nirvana and Shangri-La. A ship of hope to navigate this marbled blue planet to bring its message to individuals and the masses. But the storm of reality has dashed my ship on the rocky shoals of realism.

Faith
Once again the cats and I watch through our window in thought-filled silence the annual last dance of the leaves as they fall. With that comes the feeling of anticipated joy a new birth will bring to those who remain to witness next spring. I am content with this solace and embrace whatever lies ahead.

Charity?

Always have I felt going through life as an observer, never a participant. Forever in my dreams I see myself outside the restaurant window, observing the activities inside of the occupants so unaware of me.

Absurdities spoken from the mouth of absurdity.

WHO ARE YOU TO JUDGE?

The judge mentalists are coming! The judge mentalists are coming!

Quick are they to pull their subjective trigger on sight and sounds!

I quickly put on my suit of armor and helmet of self-esteem.

So long it took to get it, and such a price I had to pay!

I hear the drums now and the marching of the multitude drawing closer. I wipe off the sweat of anxiety on my brow and ready myself to deflect their arrows as I stand fast knowing I'll make a good accounting before I fall. I will slay their hounds.

They will hear my triumphant laugh as I remember younger days on the seas without a raft at the mercy of these clowns.

ADELANTO

Have the confidence of your convictions.
Choose what your heart tells you is right, then go for it.
Never let the naysayers into the equation.
Let your conscience be your guide and God be the judge.
No one has felt the fit of your footwear.
Nor have they walked the route of your journey.

FROM MY HAMMOCK

Gazing skyward up through the forest canopy, with senses on alert, I see the swaying movement of treetop branches at the will and whim of the orchestrated breezes.

Choreographed dance routines on a ballroom floor reflecting sunlight rays shimmering to highlight the various designs of leaves, each unique to the multicultural participants.

So unique this perspective seldom studied in such detail against panoramic background of sky blue and cloud white.

Following the tree trunks downward, I hear and see the barking squirrels as they once again prove to be the premier aerialists of the forest with aerobatic movements that defy gravity. Especially when applauded by their audience of twittering cardinals and the harsh guffaws of raucous blue jays.

I gaze in curiosity at the twisting and turning routes of countless wisteria vines coiling in every direction in its sunward quest. Ascending from tree to tree, enveloping all in an instinctive odyssey to survive.

Where is the Creator, the Supreme Power? Some go to church, synagogue, or mosque. I find HIM here in my hammock in the woods.

HAPPINESS

Happiness should be collateral; never should it be sought directly, for if that is one's sole quest, it will never be found.

Rather, that happiness, the most elusive stimuli of perception to the senses of human beings, comes to us in dribs and drabs.

Flashes of intensity that are the result of giving of ourselves to another without thought of being recompensed, be it material or emotional.

Happiness is multifaceted. It can affect all the senses of human perception. It is also the least encountered in life, thus the amazement and satisfaction when it does.

INEVITABILITY

The shadows grow longer and the light dimmer.

The springs and summers shorter and the winters longer.

Gracefully we acknowledge the inevitable as we relinquish the vitality of youth, year by year, drop by drop.

The shackles of age ever slowly erode the mind and body once so indomitable. What's left of the warrior who said, "I can"?

All is being replaced with the larger realistic perspectives from my growing vantage point as I see the big picture growing larger still.

Knowing the perpetual cycle, that great common denominator of all life, brings, at long last, serenity.

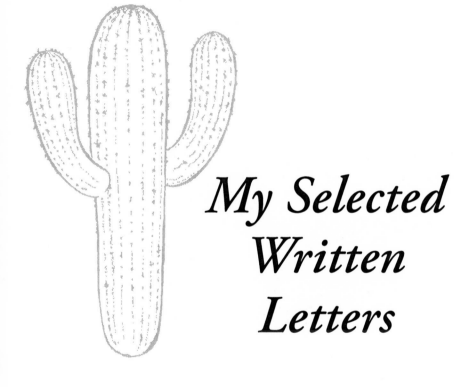

My Selected
Written
Letters

ARTHUR: REST IN PEACE

January 2, 2017

I would like to offer something to help my brother and sister in their darkest hours of this day of remembrance.

Hope is better than the misery of despair. Liberate them from anger, regret, resentment, and the inconsolable pain of loss experienced in the 2,190 days, the 52,560 hours since Arthur went to someplace we have never been before.

Gift them a miracle. Faith that all in time will be well. Give them peace. Remind them that until the time comes, their presence here means so much. It is the whole world that encompasses two young boys especially.

Yes, Sidney and Gwen, you both will always remain someone to so many. That is the destiny and responsibility you were born to. And whether or not it is clear to you, the universe is unfolding as it should. Therefore, be at peace with God, Jehovah, whatever you conceive HIM to be.

With love,
Charlie and Terri

MY DEAR GRANDCHILD

December 9, 2016

To my dearest grandchild, Jessica Marie:

I will not be around to talk to you always, so please listen to me now.

Throughout your life you will have good days and bad. You will meet people, both good and evil. I want you to learn to recognize that life is not always fair and most times we do not get what we want. Success takes very hard work and much focused energy.

Remember that we all have a boss that eventually we will have to reconcile with, the biggest being God, who will judge us all in the end.

Throughout your life you will always reap whatever it is you sow. When you plant weed seed, that is what will grow up. If you plant a flower seed, that is what will emerge from the earth. Some call it karma; whatever it is, I know it exists. It is the one common denominator of all humanity and will occur for some in this lifetime and, for others, after their death.

Do not always listen to or follow the next person. Learn to have the knowledge to know what is good and what is bad. Always do the good thing, regardless of what others do or say. Be true to yourself and your values, as we have tried to teach you.

When you give others anger, you will receive anger in return from them. When you respect others, most people, but not all, will respect you in return. There is a time to talk and a time to remain silent. I have seen people hurt as severely with the ill-spoken word coming from a hot, angry, sharp tongue than even some I have witnessed on the battlefield!

Treat all people just the way you would like them to treat you, and your days will be more peaceful and will become more pleasant and focused. Someone once said, "Muddied waters can only be cleared if left alone." Remember that!

Never forget that not everyone is your friend. There are and always will be both good and evil persons in this world. So take the time to be silent so you can observe and learn to recognize what is good and what is evil. Remember, all your actions have responsibilities and consequences to them that will affect your life and the lives of those around you.

Remember that some business is your own personal domain and needs to stay within you or at home. So once again, you must learn the value of silence to protect yourself from others that would use that against you. Life is a learning process every day, my dear granddaughter. If you need comfort or advice, go to someone who loves and cares for you that, you have learned through acquaintance and years, has no hidden agenda. They say blood is thicker than water, so I suppose that is true to an extent. Advice sometimes, I think, is like mud: ball it up and throw it against the barn wall, and anything that sticks to it might be worth keeping. Anything left is of no value to you, ignore it. You be the judge and your conscience will be your guide.

I have no doubt, dearest Jessica, that you will succeed and are capable of any goal you are willing to persevere and make whatever sacrifices necessary to achieve. It will not be easy; if that were the case, everyone would be at that plateau. Enough for now.

Perhaps, on a more subjective level, I am trying to vindicate my existence in this life? I only know that I have to make every effort to pass on to my only grandchild who will carry into the future the totality of the essence that is me and the lessons I have learned mostly through the proverbial school of hard knocks. Enough for now. I tend to ramble on when my emotions and memory get stirred! Just hoping some of this sticks to the barn wall for you.

G/pa Charlie

LETTER TO OBAMA

July 2016

President Obama:

As more and more of these most egregious recent events unfold on the television, I feel compelled to write these words to you knowing as I do you will never read them, as your staffers round file all negative or opposing points of view when addressed to you by the lowest form of life in your exalted world, the inconsequential citizen on the street.

More as a form of self-therapy than anything else during these most horrendous times, I just wanted to fantasize that I could voice my opinion to you in person the following feelings of my hopelessness in regards to the state of my country, which I love so much.

Being seventy years of age, a Vietnam combat vet, a taxpayer, and a law abider, I simply want to make this observation of you during your closing tenure as POTUS.

Your legacy, in the minds of many of my generation, will be that of someone who, despite their best intentions, has consistently struck the wrong chord with the people. Most of your knee-jerk public pronouncements in the media to the broad spectrum of folks that make up these currently not Untied States only fuel the fire! Why not let the dust settle and facts come to light?

Frankly, in my opinion, and that of many of my generation who did vote for you in 2007 believing in your mantra that better things would come and transparency, etc., I realized quite early in your first term that you were not the leader I thought you to be. Nothing more than a politician who happened to be in the right place at the right time and had an excellent vocabulary. Hearing your political mantra or stump speech for the first few times had taken this old man off guard. You will thankfully be obliged to leave in January. Behind your eight divisive years in office, nothing but broken promises of WHAT MIGHT HAVE BEEN will be left to the winds of time.

I had hoped you would not have become the egotistical and unrealistic man refusing to compromise. I wish you had not turned your back on us but rather had taken the initiative to know the difficulties of life your constituents face on a daily basis in this ever-changing world of peril and distrust that we wake up to every day. I suppose a life in academia can account for your worldly perceptions. But that does not excuse you.

Not to ramble on, President Obama, but I will close my therapy session now after these last two points. The transfer of Islamic radical terrorists from the Guantanamo detention center to freedom in foreign countries and the ability to rejoin their former ranks in the killing of American soldiers and so many other innocent civilians is beyond the pale and deeply resented by all who have served.

Your impromptu proclamations in today's civil unrest are once again so divisive and biased you do nothing but fuel the fire, as said before.

Enough said. You haven't ever changed in seven and a half years, so to think you will do so now is nothing but absurd speech from the mouth of absurdity.

Most sincerely,
Charles James Brown

JESSICA'S GRADUATION

includes "Desiderata" by Max Ehrmann
May 27, 2016

DESIDERATA
by Max Ehrmann, 1927

Go placidly amid the noise and haste, and remember what peace there may be in silence. As far as possible without surrender, be on good terms with all persons.

Speak your truth quietly and clearly; and listen to others, even the dull and the ignorant; they too have their story.

Avoid loud and aggressive persons, they are vexations to the spirit. If you compare yourself with others, you may become vain and bitter, for always there will be greater and lesser persons than yourself.

Enjoy your achievement as well as your plans. Keep interest in your career, however humble, it is a real possession in the changing fortunes of time.

Exercise caution in your business affairs for the world is full of trickery. But let this not blind you to what virtue there is; many persons strive for high ideals, and everywhere life is full of heroism.

Be yourself, especially do not feign affection. Neither be cynical about love; for in the face of all aridity and disenchantment, it is as perennial as the grass.

Take kindly the counsel of the years, gracefully surrendering the things of youth. Nurture strength of spirit to shield you in youth, nurture strength of spirit to shield you in sudden misfortune. But do not distress yourself with dark imaginings. Many fears are born of fatigue and loneliness.

Beyond a wholesome discipline, be gentle with yourself. You are a child of the universe, no less than the trees and the stars; you have a right to be here. And whether or not it is clear to you the universe is unfolding as it should. Therefore, be at peace with God, whatever you conceive Him to be. And whatever your labors and aspirations, in the noisy confusion of life, keep peace in your soul. With all its sham, drudgery and broken dreams, it is still a beautiful world. Strive to be happy.

My dearest Jessica:

I was asked to contribute an inspirational narrative in lieu of your upcoming high school graduation. I began to think about a myriad of inspirational platitudes, rhetoric, etc., I could bring forth and lay at your feet but chose instead the above treasure, the "Desiderata" by Max Ehrmann, written in 1927. I only wish I had discovered this gem earlier in my lifetime instead of after my journey through this thing called life is almost completed. Stay as true as possible to its tenets, and you will reap rewards beyond any you can imagine in this present day when you and all your classmates view the world through the rose colored glasses of young adulthood during the start of your journey today.

I share the joy and eagerness of your graduating class of 2016!

I want you all to dream the impossible dream, joust the windmills, and slay the dragons of man's inhumanity to man.

Make this a better world for all, because the graduating class of Chattahoochee High School is determined to persevere starting on May 27, 2016. God bless and protect all of you in your quest.

With love you will never know the extent of.

Blessed with only one grandchild, Jessica Marie Zdenek.

What I lack in quantity is made up tenfold in the quality you have, Jessie.

Your G/pa,
Charlie James Brown

WHERE HAVE ALL THE PATRIOTS GONE?

November 12, 2015

To: All GOP representatives of "We the people"
Subject: Where have all the patriots gone?

Why can't our elected representatives hold the line of containment on this divisive POTUS Obama and his stooges in these last months of his waning tenure? Knowing full well he is hell-bent in his insatiable compulsion to destroy or redefine the standards and traditions, Constitution and Bill of Rights, hopes and dreams that have held this country united for 239 years.

"We will die trying" is his mantra. What is the G.O.P. doing? From the cities and towns, villages and farmlands, coast to coast, citizens are beyond frustration; they are outraged at a "do NOTHING" strategy prevalent in the Senate, House, and judiciary that refuses to defend checks and balances of governmental authority. Federal bureaucracy has obliterated state rights in a tsunami of presidential and unlawful edicts and proclamations!

Quite frankly, this delusional POTUS has been allowed to regress these once-united states fifty years! He has burnt all the bridges and polarized the people at home and abroad.

Stop the political infighting and the self-reinforcing cycle of political correctness to gain media attention! Make every effort to achieve a goal of "MY country must and will be first." You must bring this message across the aisle. Prove to us PATRIOTS still exist on Capitol Hill. If ever there is a time for all good men and women to come to the aid of their country, it is NOW or NEVER! My country is under siege!

Charles J. Brown

SENATOR ISAKSON

July 2014

Honorable Johnny Isakson:

You and your fellow Republicans are the last bastion of hope that we, the people, can turn to for help, at least until November, when we will send you the cavalry in the form of control of the Senate.

You and everyone else in the United States, except the ultra-elitist Far Left and those who have personal and political things to gain, know that we have the most incompetent and vengeful president in the history of this country.

Our latest scandal and crisis exist in our own backyard in the form of a mass exodus of illegals crossing at will into our sovereign territory while our so-called leader shoots pool and drinks beer in Colorado and, without a doubt, could care less! We, the people, are suffering under his two terms of reckless irresponsibility. With his usual lack of common sense, he laughs at us with his photo ops, complete with background of schoolchildren and young people that could not answer any pertinent question about our history or Constitution. He acts like a stand-up comedian about the troubles, foreign and domestic, he has plunged us into. He spent his whole life not in the real world but in the lap of academia, where he feels most at ease with the young and uninformed, where he is praised like the rock star he thinks he is. Enough!

I will end my ramble now. I want you to gather all allies in the House and Senate, including those increasing number of common-sense members now deserting this sinking ship from the other side of the aisle, and change the immigrant law passed in 2008 to include not just illegal children from Mexico and Canada but all children, regardless of country of origin, that have nefariously cloaked themselves as refugees of oppression in order to circumvent the law as now written and gain access to our country and its "freebies," which must be addressed at a later date.

Furthermore, the useless functions of the United Nations and its members must be prodded off their duffs to do what they can. This useless collection of hypocrites must also be addressed at a later date.

Mexico and its president, Nieto, must be warned in no uncertain terms that if they continue to allow free passage of these illegals from its small 135-mile border with Guatemala and provide trains to facilitate their movement, they must STOP immediately! If not, we must grow testicles big enough to at last stop this invasion of our country with ALL OPTIONS available. *All* means including closing the border, urging a tourist boycott, and encouraging the suspension of all NAFTA trade and aid to what we ridiculously call our friendly neighbors to the south. I have been married forty-six years to a lady now a US citizen formally from Hermosillo, Sonora, Mexico. She waited in line, crossed legally, learned English, held a job, and paid her taxes while raising our two bilingual children, now very productive adults with college degrees we and they themselves worked to pay for. They now contribute to society, not take from society as if it were an entitlement. I can assure you many of our Latino friends that have circumstances similar to ours are insulted by the policies that favor illegals over taxpaying citizens! This all the politicians know but choose to ignore, lest we not be politically correct and hurt the sensitivities of ILLEGAL immigrants and their advocates. This has been going on now for decades and is steadily increasing, being incentivized by Obama and bleeding-heart liberals who would have us destroyed from within if given their way.

Believe me, Johnny, this letter is not the ranting of an old senior citizen, but the words based on the sixty-seven years I have observed the loss of our freedoms. I am the voice of a vast majority of people I encounter these days, veterans like myself who would once again bear arms and the silent majority who, at long last, are speaking out in public places, churches, stores, town hall meetings, etc.

We, the people, cannot stand any more of the Obama lack of leadership and veracity! The IRS, CIA, DOJ, V.A., Benghazi, Iraq, Afghanistan, fast and furious, Syria, Ukraine, and shovel ready jobs. Too big to fail bailouts, tremendous amounts of "stimulus" money that went where? The decimation of our troops and air and armed forces at their lowest levels since pre-WWII. The boneheaded, treasonous actions that trade five top Taliban prisoners to gain one U.S. Army deserter and consequently have killed all morale and no doubt will result in further deaths to our young men, and now women, who serve at the front!

Now we are being invaded on our own domestic soil, and all that idiot can say is "Give me 3.7 billion dollars in emergency spending so I can help these poor children," while we at home cannot even help our own homeless and starving—yes, starving—children.

The blame can be shared by the GOP also! One vacation after another in these times of crisis CANNOT be justified by any spin. I would convey that to your colleagues in most strong terms. We will not hesitate to vote out of office any and all, if necessary, that cannot do the job of protecting this country TODAY! Time is not on our side. Stop talking and roll up your sleeves and DO SOMETHING constructive to protect our hemorrhaging country and its lawful citizens! You all were sent to Washington, DC, to WORK for us; if not, we will do whatever is necessary to do it for you, and all who refuse can starting packing their luggage NOW!

Most very sincerely,
Your very discouraged constituent, Mr. Charles James Brown

AN OPEN LETTER TO THE AMERICAN VOTER

April 23, 2013

Bumbling, stumbling, groping, and clueless, this nation, without a viable and credible chief executive and administration, continues their amateurish and blind, on-the-job experiment in their quite sad and oftentimes comic journey at our expense, while the clock of tenure approaches the three-fourths mark in this pitiful sojourn to the blessed point of termination at last.

Eight wasted years preceded by sixteen previous years of a milder form of the same disease. Twenty-four years on the decline will be a harder hurdle to overcome, if even possible. Those of us who lived in a much less-restrictive atmosphere of liberty, more honest, self-supporting, more innovative, stronger, and globally respected as a nation, are nothing but a voice in the wind now. Our numbers are decreasing year by year, and the newer generations have nothing to compare with, most too busy with social and political correctness to even imagine or learn the history of their own country. Some to the point of not even using or caring for the blood and treasure spent on their privilege to vote! They cannot fathom, nor have they even the curiosity to listen to the few elders left that remember a much-better America past. When I said "comic journey," it is only metaphoric, as the reality today is anything but; it is a damn shame we allowed this divisiveness we live in to happen! We, the people, have the right to send to Washington, DC, those people we vote for to serve us faithfully and honestly and never let them forget that!

The wounds inflicted upon this land that God once shed his grace upon will take decades to heal, if at all. When will we ever learn to vote for the core constitutional values of the Founding Fathers? Is this the heartfelt words of a candidate on stage asking for our vote, or is it political foible being spoken as scripted for more secret and nefarious agendas?

It is up to an informed citizenry to ferret out the person's background, history, and character to the best of their abilities. This is not a popularity contest, a music talent show, or even a stand-up comic contest we are voting for, so cast your votes responsibly for you will live with the consequences. How many times must we be forced to choose between bad and worse, truth-teller or liar, competent or inept, patriot or actor at the ballot box? In 2016 we must come prepared and not keep handing the keys of the people's kingdom and power to the usurpers and socialists that are openly, actively, and arrogantly rearranging the face of this once-great beacon of light now dimmed to the fates of Athens and Rome.

Now is the time for all good men and women to wake up and come to the aid of their country!

CJB

LETTER TO HOME DEPOT: SEPTEMBER 2010

September 1, 2010

September 1, 2010

Dear Mr. Frank at Home Depot:

I moved here to Georgia after thirty-eight years in California just five years ago. I bought a home very much in need of repair. Needless to say, I quickly became a good customer of your store with all its courteous and professional associates. I have literally spent thousands of dollars at this facility.

One of the most rewarding and impressive feelings I enjoyed about my "candy store" was the fact that they honored the service of military personnel, both active and retired, with a very much appreciated 10 percent discount. How honored I felt that the management of Home Depot would give recognition to the sacrifices of the military! A rare and wonderful thing.

Well, all that came to an abrupt and sudden end this Monday past, when I visited your store. They rescinded, as you must know, all 10 percent discounts to Veterans Day only. Why did you all honor us so and then apparently, during these hard economic times, slam it closed in our faces for the God Almighty profit margin even though you have steadily raised prices to compensate for this during the time frame beginning eighteen months ago?

I was a navy corpsman. An FMF veteran who was assigned to assist the U.S.M.C. I participated in seven amphibious landings, a total of fifteen months in First Corp area from Chu-Lai north to the DMZ. Wishing you and others could witness the absolute courage of the young men we send into harm's way and the incomprehensible carnage that high-velocity metal can inflict upon human anatomy! I had joined up immediately upon my seventeenth birthday to escape foster homes and grew up fast! No big deal. When I did finally return to the West Coast my fellow Vietnam vets and I received the jeers, howls, and garbage thrown at us by a GRATEFUL NATION in protest. So we old goats of Vietnam are really used to the crap Home Depot just delivered to us. Thank goodness I personally do not need your 10 percent discount! You can stick it where the sun does not shine!

It's the young men, and now women, on active duty, serving in countries to protect you and your chance at the free enterprise system that really stinks!

I, for one, no matter what, will never again step a foot inside a Home Depot store. I have started urging, all my fellow veteran friends still alive, and also the military organizations and reunions I attend, the military families to boycott your stores nationwide. I will devote whatever time is left of me to fulfill that goal.

If you never intended to honor us, why did you initiate that policy, to begin with? Ignorance is bliss. Your competitors made no such false show of support, to begin with. I personally feel, when someone extends something to someone under these circumstances, they are twice as culpable when they, without warning or explanation in advance, just rescind it!

I hope your financial strategy backfires, profit margins plunge, and chapter 11 becomes your fate. I only wish to God I could return life to the 58,479 heroes of Vietnam as fast as you jerked us around. That includes the 4,200 KIA in Iraq and 1,800 KIA in Afghanistan to say nothing of the soldiers permanently maimed so you all can get that extra dollar of pure profit! My biggest wish of all, though it will never come to pass, is to have had the profiteer who made this decision in a foxhole with me forty-six years ago! Thanks! Before you round file this, do you have the COURAGE to let Mr. Blank and Mr. Arthur see this? I would like their response but will not hold my breath—silence speaks volumes! I believe I already have the answer to that one. In the words of your associate in the garden department after telling me the news, "Have a nice day now."

Charlie James Brown

NOTE: Very soon after this letter, Home Depot clarified its discount policy to active military and veterans for all stores in Georgia to extend the discount 365 days of the year. To this day, I enjoy my shopping experiences there! I have met many veterans employed by Home Depot, and on behalf of all, I salute them!

LETTER TO OBAMA

March 17, 2009

President Obama:

Absolute Insanity in Government—AIG! For you and those clowns in the financial circus you are running to allow these criminals who ought to be in jail or on death row to steal our money is insanity. Why the big rush to push this absurd debt on us? Amateurish politics at best. If it were not so pitiful seeing our beloved country going down the drain, it might almost be as funny as watching a rerun of the Keystone Kops.

To think that I voted for you and relied, as many did, on what appeared to be a vehicle for a transparent change in government. Well, the joke appears to be on me and on all those poor souls who believed in you. Fire that treasury secretary who did not even pay his income taxes, and yet you felt he was such an asset! I have never seen such a debacle—and I thought G. W. was disorganized!

I have lost all faith in your ability to accomplish anything. You open your mouth to appease us with all the rhetoric, and you don't even have a logical plan A or B thought out (i.e., Gitmo). Maybe we should send these worst of the worst of combat terrorists to a halfway house in Illinois, while their comrades overseas continue to kill and behead our courageous troops? Better check with the ACLU first, though. President Barack Obama, please clean up your house and surround yourself with better and more knowledgeable people to assist you.

By the way, what has "Sheriff" Joe Biden been doing lately since pimping his ride home on Amtrak for a billion dollars? While you are at it, tell Ms. Pelosi to buy her own plane. Dodd, Murtha, and Barney Frank will be voted out along with her when they come up for re-election. Maybe in one of these elections we, the people, will get some experienced leadership. Per usual, your staff will probably round file this negative letter, but hopefully enough, citizens who feel just like I do will let you know that we need a change we can believe in.

Desperately seeking better change,
Charles J. Brown

NOTE: AIG is the American International Group. The Obama administration approved a bailout of more than 170 billion dollars to them in taxpayer money from the treasury and Federal Reserve. AIG then went on to pay out 165 million dollars in bonuses to its executives!

LETTER TO OBAMA

March 8, 2009

Dear Mr. President:

Please refrain from media attention to your lavish Wednesday evening dinners at the White House. At least close the door and don't shove it in our faces during these critical economic times. I, for one, find it most distasteful. Pun intended. These are not visiting foreign state diplomats you are hosting.

You are now about to sign that pig's-ear-filled congressional funding bill. This goes against everything you told us, which is beginning to become a familiar trend, in your first fifty days of tenure. I voted for you down here, contrary to all my friends calling you another silver-tongued politician, because I really believed in you, heart and soul.

The only thing I saw missing on that publicized, most expensive, tax-dollar-paid menu was PORK. If that is in short supply at your house, I suggest contacting Pelosi, Reid, Dodd, or Barney Frank and the swine herd they wallow with who have been feeding at the public trough for way too long.

"Change you can believe in" indeed! It's nothing but business as usual, looking up from the bottom-rail boss man.

Sincerely,
Charles J. Brown

My Personally Written Poems

REMEMBERING ARTHUR

January 2, 2017

Taken from us much too soon, so suddenly without a chance to say goodbye,
so many achievements, yet vast potential still untapped.
His book barely half-written, race barely begun, now leaving us so forlorn we mourn, we cry.
Years later, still when these holidays chill, like the gifts lying there still unwrapped.
We must take solace in our faith, that we shall meet once more.
In a land beyond the rainbow, on a distant shore.

CANDLEWICK AND TEARS

January 2016

When we lose one loved so dearly, bitterest tears are called forth by the memory or hours spent when we loved not enough.
The flame extended from its umbilical wick.
Barely had the wax beads begun their descending melt,
when an errant gust of air from nowhere was felt.
Looking back at the cylindrical spire, only a wisp of smoke ascended,
the delicate balance of life so young incomprehensively ended.
Gone too soon, the many I have counted.
Gone, on celestial horses mounted.
Oh, that a grand reunion be reborn,
for all the brothers, sisters, and others I do mourn.
But I have no more tears, they have all been shed,
enough for my eternity and beyond to last.
Dry as the barren desert sands, the place I lay my head.
No visible sign of unfathomable sorrow felt when they had past.
Alone now with only thoughts of how hard it would have been to say goodbye.
Yet it was harder still when I refused to say it.
Surrendering to the things I could not change when at first I saw or heard they would die.
Tears all gone, reservoir empty, here in this valley of tears I wait.

DANGEROUS LEE

January 2016

The years fly by now as if on wings of birds in swift flight, escaping the hunters that come with the night. Still always I muse with warmth and glow when some young men I used to know came together and bonded that summer so many years ago.

They stood strong, knowing no fear. Daring life's challenges with an invincible swagger, a laugh, and a beer. Faded memories now burning in the embers low. This old man looking in the mirror at someone I hardly recognize although I should know.

But we all remember that special day in September. The long journey made carrying all that pain. Doctors had warned him his injuries were many and his last days were few, with none left to gain. He would be a dead man at age forty-two.

But then again, never did they know the Lee that we knew. He had never bent to fight the unbeatable foe. To be at his firstborn daughter's wedding, the father valiantly did go.

When he gave you his word, it was better than gold, no matter the price. So his last days were spent at this blessed event. To fulfill his promise and throw some rice. Never was Dangerous Lee ever intimidated to not roll the dice!

Though it threw him in the fast lane, losing many talents he was born with, a toolbox with all the tools! Going to the edge, once too often placing himself in harm's way. Experiencing life to the fullest, always in a hurry to see around the bend, when he neared the end, he lost a couple of friends. A career once so promising now broken by the white powder that froze his charisma to ice as the habit extends.

Gathering up the last of his strength, when the festivities ended, he set forth. On his way back up north, somewhere around the Fisherman's Wharf. I just know he saw the sun set for him one last time, over his blue Pacific Ocean, just as he had intended.

Two days later, it came as no surprise when word came back that he had been found sitting stone-cold dead in his seat at the back of that old Greyhound. My dear brother Lee, I will always recall and see our many adventures in time so brief and short. Like a ship sunk on a reef before leaving its port.

I, being much older, should have been more assertive and bolder. I was your friend. I should have stuck with you closer. I should have been your shadow to see the light and avoid this end. Gone way too soon. With so much unfulfilled potential, the graveyard now strewn.

Gone forever amid the stars and the moon. But in the hush of a quiet summer's night, I can hear his laughter so loud. I see the red hair tousled, remember the brother riding a Harley, singing that tune. I remember those days standing together in our crowd, when we all felt rock-hard and so damn proud.

NEVER WILL THEY LEARN

2016

Ink stains dried to bloodstains on the blotter. Another page of history was written. The latest generation of youth was led to slaughter.

For democracy and equality, rant the politicians from their seaside villas' vacation. Lives lost, so filled with potential, ground to cannon fodder. What? Who? Where? When? Why? Anguished cries rise from the masses to those chosen to lead this nation.

Little do they know, nothing do they care. Waiting at the podium, wondering about how they will look with what they wear and "How's my hair?" "Hurry up, teleprompter and camera lights," under their breath they swear. Golf course awaits with dinner there and only an hour to spare.

When once again these lavishly appareled jackals, without the slightest pause or hesitation or the dignity of a whore, will face camera right and empathetically declare transgressions, real or imaged, as they send another generation off to war.

History pages thicken with those stricken; another soldier dies as the ink blotter dries.

CAT CATHARSIS

2015

Give me cats to grow old with.
Amuse and enchant the lonely hours, dispel that old myth.
Cats to mellow my mood.
These golden years, now upon me, can be so rude and crude.
Felines of many colors with eyes of rainbow hues.
Without my little lions' pride, this world we built together would be a pitiful ruse.
But now I can smile at the inevitable, with three friends at my side.
Each with a personality so unique in tandem, with a sleek and graceful glide.
Watching them climb to attain the pinnacle of that old rocking chair.
Content now am I to ponder untenable, peace filled somethings in that beautiful, piercing stare.

SAPLING

2015

At last the long-awaited day, the candle only burns one way.
A sapling born of the seed of its DNA.
A tree now grown through the decades in the protection of the forest isolation.
Never will it experience the ax of man or civilization—what a joyous revelation!
Only the cycle of nature's elements to ever touch, shape, weather, break, and renew as meant to be.
Sometimes I wish I could be such a tree.

ODE TO SOUTH VIETNAM

2010

To my final resting place I will go, through these past decades I did with so many memories grow. No matter what, no matter where, I did my best for many that really don't care.

But always, my brothers, though memory may fade, your names now, it is your youthful faces I still see so clear in that long-ago country that gave no cheer. In my memories of sacrifices given so dear. We will forever remain there with our youth intact. As somehow a tribute to valor and act. Your honor and courage even in orders we thought not so sage, we did our duty, and as is said, some gave their all.

Many years later, before I fall, always will I see us standing so tall, with the pride of tradition and never an act of sedition or contrition as we walked down that jungle trail. Where, in the end, I do not pretend but revere the ultimate sacrifice you gave for all. If they now care to see, placed proudly is your name on that black marble wall, for that became your destiny when you answered the call.

Charles J. Brown, former U.S. Navy corpsman, 1964–1968
Served in First Corps area, Republic of South Vietnam, 1965–1967

TWO YOUNG MEN AND THE SEA

2014

Back then so long ago, we were invincible, would live and love forever and a day,
But like sand through the hourglass, the years just sifted away.
Washed ashore like driftwood now in some unknown bay.
Creased with wrinkles and scarred throughout, the salty breeze blowing through hair and beards of gray.
Bowed old heads as we amble aimlessly, can barely detect the smiles concealed,
because we both know we did it all our own way!

Note: The other young man of the sea being Dr. Sidney S. Bernstein.

DREAMIN'

2009

To write a word, to sing a song,
to lift one's spirit as the day grows long.

To tell a joke, to laugh a laugh,
to ply one's trade in building that raft.

To float down the river and watch things go by,
to dream my dreams and touch the sky.

Never do I want this journey to end.
Current running strong now as I round the bend.

Revealing the destination I knew would come.
Dreams destroyed by reality, only a romantic like me,
could be so dumb.

JESTER

2008

Like the four seasons, I come and I go.
Trying hard to leave a trail of smiles,
or even a seed of thought planted that's meant to grow.

No court or king to weigh me down,
I am free to ply my trade and act the clown.

Laughter's anesthesia to dull the pain.
Raindrops in cadence, kittens, puppies, and
comets to ease the strain.

TELL ME SO

2008

This I see as I watched it grow.
Through all these years at least I know.
I just needed someone to tell me so.
Hang me high or hang me low.
Just affirm that I did exist.
My worst fear would be the answer: no.

ESCAPE

2007

Sensitivities trampled beyond the measure,
Feelings bludgeoned that no longer exist.
Never more will grow this earthly treasure,
of tender thoughts never kissed.
They can never imagine all they have missed.
Heart bruised beyond repair.
I am a fool to dream they care,
a bigger one yet to even sit and despair.
Let down the drawbridge as I ride through the breech.
Let loose that urn, free my spirit to soar,
to a place never more within their reach.

ARE YOU THERE?

2006

God, you made this world with all its beauty and wonder.
Filled it with life so diverse on lands that rise and fall.
Skies blue, clouds white or dark with thunder.
Oceans wide and waves so tall, yet despite your birth in a manger's stall,
mankind still refuses to heed your call.
Wars so endless blood saturates the earth, marking spots where the
broken bodies fell.
Innocents dying every day with their backs to the wall.
Why, oh, why, Lord, have you let our earth turn into hell?
Without even a lift of a finger, you could break this spell.
Am I to believe you have forsaken them all?
Not for me do I make this plea.
My time and others past have been winnowed into chaff.
But I think of babes in arms and those to be.
Somewhere in that great book of prophecy.
Spoke of a time of rewards and a fatted calf.
Is that just another promise made broken in half?

LOST IN THE LAND OF MY BIRTH

2006

Build the ramparts strong and tall.
Encase the heart with layers of callouses all.
Drawbridge the soul, let that phone ring,
never answer its call.
Keep confidence in, but never outwardly confide.
Control the emotions even to those known and have died.
Freeze out the love, never let that thaw.
for as sure as the sun in the east does rise,
it will be no surprise,
like the hawk kills the dove,
if the ice melts, it will be the eventual demise,
of a fool drowned in the ocean of emotion
so bloody and raw.

IN THE STILLNESS OF THE NIGHT

March 1992

In the stillness of a quiet summer's night,
one can let the mind wander through memories of past life
that come to light.
Old thoughts and experiences brew in the cauldron of the
subconscious and bubble over in awesome recognition,
As the rivers of memories cascade into consciousness.
Some are remembered with contrition,
while others with a smile I greet as old friends long lost
found at last!

MISS FOX

November 1964

Written by Charles J. Brown while attending U.S.N. Hospital Corps, "A" school at Great Lakes NTC in Michigan. Lieutenant Commander Fox, USN Nurse Corps, veteran of WWII, was in charge of our coed class, Company 8, that graduated in November 1964. This is dedicated to her humanity and empathy for all of us.

M   is for our mothers you remind us of.

I   is for the interwoven ways you've shown your love.

S   is for the sunshine you've brought to our days.

S   is for the sacrifices made in many ways.

F   is for the finest nurse we have ever known.

O   is for that one who in our hearts has grown.

X   is for the extra things that can't be put to rhyme,
because they will always be in our memories and withstand the test of time.

SAINT PATRICK

1963

On an emerald isle in a blue sea,
a child was born to destiny.
Patrick was the name given at birth,
a name to become famous throughout the earth.

The child grew in wisdom and grace,
But was anguished to see the sins of his race.
He resolved to crusade for a godly cause,
took up the shamrock and made straight the laws.

It is said, though legend it may be,
he drove the snakes of Ireland into the sea.
But whatever he did, you may be sure,
his fame will always echo in Irish folklore.

The winds of time cannot taint,
the historic memories of that Irish saint,
and once a year his posterity pay,
their respects to him on Saint Patrick's Day.

FRIENDSHIP (KIDS' STUFF)

1962

All must have this or they'd die,
Without it life is a gloomy mist,
All must have someone to say hi,
They must have someone on their list.

Life is tolerable with a friend,
But without him you are lost,
Because in the end,
You are like a flower in the frost,
Without a friend.

MY DOG (KIDS' STUFF)

1962

Beside me he trots with his head held high,
His tail waves when I call him by name.
I smile as I see the joy in his eye.
I know I wouldn't trade him for glory or fame.
The sun comes up and warms the day,
I wake up thinking with you I'll play.
Oh, what heartbreak when I open the door
And remember you aren't with me anymore.
To hear your friendly bark again would make life such a lark.
Your face in the window, as a rule, would always greet me after school.
Your cold red tongue to give a lick.
Your eager response to catch a stick.
All these things I remember of you,
But alas, you are gone, leaving me so blue.

THE LIFE OF THE LAND

1962

Winter swoops down like a bird of the night,
Gripping the land in its icy talons,
Wrapping its victims in wings of white.

As time flies on, the raptor will depart,
The winds will soften their howls to a whisper,
And spring will return the land to its heart.

Green buds sprout flowers both common and rare,
While flora and fauna tend to their young,
Summer dwells in the land with nary a care.

Shouting loud its warning, autumn shortens the light,
The leaves wither and die in deadly fear,
Land awaits the return of the bird of the night.

THOUGHTS

1962

For years upon years that tree had stood,
Through times of wet and dry,
Its struggle for life in the greenwood,
Might bring tears to the eye.

From seed to sprout it had fought,
The elements from which it came,
In old age it found the peace it had sought,
Though it was death that was to blame.

SPARE ME THIS SIGHT

1961
my first poem to commemorate the Civil War Centennial,
aged fourteen

Down in the valley I saw their lines,
One of blue, the other gray.
I saw the smoke rise from the pines,
I heard the cannon roar that day.

The columns clashed, many cries I heard,
But the battle still raged on.
Then the gray line broke and through vision blurred,
I watched until they had gone.

When all had passed and silence reigned,
Upon that charred and bloodied field,
I revered the ground as sacred, by blood ordained,
And in reverent awe I kneeled.

I prayed that henceforth I can be spared,
This day's most horrible sight,
That of countrymen and brothers paired,
On a battlefield in mortal fight.

My Personally Written Short Stories

BROOKLYN ROSE

January 1, 2017

I watched the dervish dancing of autumn leaves across the wide asphalt avenue. I imagined them to be in synchronized rhythm with music of wind chimes coming from several porch fronts along the long row of houses. All this being set into motion and orchestrated by the steady flow of a southwest breeze.

No one in the neighborhood, not even the oldest residents, could remember who might have planted the rosebush or any circumstance leading to its origin.

For at least seventy years, that huge red climbing rose, with the original canes now the diameter of small trees, had been a fixture in the vacant lot at the northeast corner of Atlantic and Washington Avenues. Some say it was meant to be, that the cracked concrete provided protection and the clay and soil it nourishes from contributed to the vigorous growth. Had it not been for the adjacent Acme advertisement billboard sign that eventually became its trellis and support system, the tenacious climbing rose would never have survived to attain the size and local fame it now enjoys.

The Brooklyn rose overcame a challenge presented some forty years ago when a city ordinance was approved banning all billboards in that area. A waiver of exemption was granted for this particular site, or perhaps I should say it was a diplomatic way to quell anger and outcry from the local residents thinking their Brooklyn rose landmark might be threatened or possibly lost. The Acme Company, of course, no longer pastes advertisements on its sign but had agreed in writing to donate their property with the billboard and framework that has been completely encapsulated by the rose to the point where they now appear to be monolithic!

For over seven decades, this queen of all roses has witnessed the ebb and flow of the lives of people coming and going. Think of the progression of births, marriages, and funeral processions that have passed by the Brooklyn rose in its long span of existence. Photographs that immortalized the participants of special events with Brooklyn rose serving as background can no doubt be found in the albums of many local homes.

The multitude of thousands of fragrant medium-sized bloodred rose blooms welcoming yet another spring and summer have now attracted many folks from near and far. Rumor has it that NYC has officially designated our rose as a landmark and that postcards with its image are being sold in gift shops throughout the metro area.

Another aspect of this Brooklyn lady that is seldom mentioned is the nurturing she has provided throughout her lifetime. Many a sparrow, starling, and pigeon began life in nests amid the tangled sheltering tentacles of glossy green leaves with thorns to protect and pierce any who might transgress the sanctuary she gifted.

The fragrance emulating from the regal red robes of this magnificent monarch has been known to attract hundreds of butterflies, ladybugs, and hummingbirds of all varieties. Some say that her perfume may even be detected as far as Greenpoint when conditions and the northern breeze are just right.

How many buds and blooms from Brooklyn rose have adorned prom queens, Mother's Day recipients, baby showers, and the various multitudes of vases adorning breakfast tables, hospital rooms, and so many other occasions throughout the years?

The oldest known rose in the world grows on the wall of the Catholic cathedral in Hildesheim, Germany. It is thirty-three feet high and thirty feet wide. Documentation verifies this wild dog rose (*Rosa canina*) at approximately seven hundred years old. Although the cathedral was bombed by the Allies in World War II, the root system remained intact, and since 1945, this tenacious and wild climbing rose has been able to survive and begin its regrowth among the ruins to the size noted above.

The largest known rosebush is located in Tombstone, Arizona. Planted in 1885, it now spans an incredible area of nine thousand square feet, and the original cane from the rootstock is twelve feet in circumference!

FLAT STANLEY TRAVELS

written for Laquetta
2007

Dear Laquetta,

Flat Stanley arrived today along with your letter and lovely photograph, thank you very much. Our adventures are about to begin. Are you ready? Here we go.

Monday: Stanley went to the San Bernardino County Fair with me. Victorville has been home to the San Bernardino County Fair for over seventy-five years now. San Bernardino County is the largest county in the United States, encompassing an area of 20,106 square miles; 90 percent of the county is desert, and the remainder consists of San Bernardino Valley and the San Bernardino Mountains.

Tuesday: Stanley and I got up extra early this morning and traveled approximately thirty-five miles northeast of Victorville to the home of an old silver-mining town near Yermo, California, called Calico Ghost Town. More than a century ago, the town of Calico was bustling with prospectors. Founded in March 1881, it grew to a population of 1,200 with twenty-two saloons and more than five hundred mines. Silver was king, and the Calico mining district became one of the richest in California, producing $86 million in silver, $45 million in borax, and of course gold. After 1907, when silver prices dropped and borax mining moved to Death Valley, Calico became a ghost town. It is now a state park, and people can visit the old town and see the buildings as they were one hundred years ago. Stanley took a picture of two tourists visiting the old Calico schoolhouse.

Wednesday, Thursday, and Friday: Our biggest and longest adventure began when Stanley wanted to explore the desert! Victorville is surrounded by a vast desert called the Mojave Desert. It is also referred to as the high desert area because of its elevation on a plateau that stretches from the Cajon Pass (elevation 4,260 feet) to the Nevada border and beyond. Stanley was surprised to learn that although it is very hot in the desert during the daytime, it gets very cold at night because the vast barren land has no forests, plant life, or other features to absorb and hold the sun's heat. Since we knew our exploring trip would take some time, we packed the Jeep with a tent and overnight camping gear and headed east, going down Seventh Street, which is Victorville's main street, which used to be part of the old Route 66. This route used to be the main US highway for people to travel from Los Angeles, California, to Chicago, Illinois, in the 1930s and 1940s. One of Stanley's first questions was, "What are the strange trees with spiked leaves?" I told him they were named Joshua trees by the early Mormon settlers as they rolled their covered wagons through this area in the late 1880s. Joshua trees are found only in the Mojave Desert. I took Stanley to the biggest one I knew of in the Victorville area, and he took my picture. Joshua trees grow slowly, and I estimated this old giant to be at least two hundred years old! We stopped for lunch in the shade of some big rocks. I told Stanley to be careful and look out for scorpions and tarantula spiders that might be hiding nearby as he sat eating his flat-egg sandwich and toothpaste cap full of milk. The rest of the day was spent driving over dry lakes of hard-packed sand that used to be full many thousands of years ago, when dinosaurs roamed what was then a vibrant-green and fertile valley. Setting up camp that night, Stanley was frightened to hear the howls from some nearby coyotes. The next day, we arrived at the Bristol Mountain Range and explored an abandoned old mine that used to produce iron ore. That afternoon, Stanley and I stopped to eat. Guess what Stanley had? You guessed it—he had another flat-egg sandwich and a toothpaste cap full of fresh milk! On our way back, we stopped at the site of an extinct volcano in Amboy,

California. As we climbed to the top of this dome, Stanley became very frightened and alarmed by the dry sound of rattling from a nearby lava ledge. I shouted for Stanley to stand still and not move! Just then, a large pale-green snake slithered by in the opposite direction. Stanley had just seen the most poisonous snake in the whole Northern Hemisphere, the deadly diamond-backed Mojave green rattlesnake! It contains two types of toxins in its poisonous venom, and its bite is almost always fatal if no antivenom is available or you are too far out in the desert for quick medical treatment. This snake is found only in the Mojave Desert. We spent an uneventful night in our camp tent, and guess what? Stanley was no longer afraid to hear the coyotes howl because he was beginning to learn that most of the desert mammals, birds, and reptiles will not harm you if you do not try to capture them or accidently step on them. We arrived home the next morning, and Stanley was still so tired from his adventures that he went to take a nap and did not help me put our camping gear away!

Saturday: Stanley and I went to see the city of Victorville's public works yard. This is where the dump trucks, backhoes, road graders, Vactor / sewer-maintenance trucks, high-lift boom trucks, asphalt rollers, and a variety of other types of equipment are kept and maintained. This machinery is used throughout the city to keep the roads cleaned and repaired and also to keep the sewers running, traffic signals working, and many other things to enable the city to function in an orderly fashion. Stanley also visited the Animal Control Department, where lost and stray dogs, cats, and other animals are picked up and cared for until new homes can be found for them or their owners claim them. Stanley saw the sign shop that makes all the street signs for the city as well, as the paint-striping truck to make the lane lines on the street. Stanley met one of the supervisors, who was pleased to give him the official seal of the city to take back to Mrs. Tennyson's class and show to all the girls and boys.

Sunday: Stanley said goodbye as we got ready to mail him back to Laquetta and the second-grade students of Mrs. Tennyson's class. As the mailman beeped his horn and before taking flat Stanley to the post office, I could only wonder where he would go on his next great adventure.

CJB

NOTE: Mrs. Sarah (Bernstein) Tennyson, a Chicago schoolteacher, is the daughter of Dr. and Mrs. Sidney Bernstein.

MYSTERY BLUE

2007

John Jacobs awoke with a sense of urgency. The first perception of his emerging consciousness was the lapping water wet against his legs and the sound of waves slapping the shore. Remembering the events of the previous week came painfully to him as he rubbed the swelling lump on his forehead and lifted his body from the sand. He felt for his wallet. The shock that came to him was expected as he realized it was missing.

He trudged through the driftwood-strewn beach and made his way to the nearly deserted highway. To his relief, he found his car as he had left it the previous evening hidden in the underbrush of creosote and mesquite. Reaching under the fender for his hidden extra key, he started the engine and instinctively steered his vehicle in the direction he was traveling when he first saw that faint blue glow on the eastern horizon. Glancing at the instrument panel, he calculated enough fuel remained to reach his destination.

Within an hour, the car ground to a halt in front of a weathered wooden building predominately displaying a red sign with large block lettering warning, "Rutherford Mining Co. Private Property. Keep Out." At that moment, John's attention was drawn to a noise at the rear of the property that marked the entrance to the main mine shaft.

With cautious strides, he rounded the corner of the building, and a noise reminiscent of the distant buzzing of bees grew louder as he approached the elevator car. Stepping inside and locking the sliding cage door, he peered downward as his eyes adjusted to the glowing blue mist emitting from the dark depths. The whirling noise of greased steel cables on pulleys merged with the ever-increasing buzzing crescendo as the meshed steel cage continued its agonizingly slow descent into the bowels of the cold mine shaft.

It had started last summer, a chance encounter with an old friend. Ralph Rutherford had once been an emerging star in their college days. Extremely intelligent, this popular, outgoing young man continually aced the geology courses. After graduation, they had drifted apart. John had gone on to pursue a law degree, and word through the grapevine had said Ralph ventured south into Mexico, where he was employed as a governmental survey geologist.

Though decades had passed, their instant recognition at an estate sale had rekindled their friendship, and an open invitation for John to visit his old schoolmate now residing on the California Gulf Coast of Western Sonora, near Kino Bay, was accepted.

Recently divorced and now semiretired, John had looked forward to this visit and escape from the high pace of his Scottsdale, Arizona, lifestyle.

Somehow, he wasn't surprised to find Ralph living on-site in the primitive confines of a rural home next to his own mine.

The ensuing days were spent mostly in the coastal resort town near Tiburón Island as John became increasingly aware of Ralph's reluctance to talk about mining on his property other than to say it was now just a hobby. John's curiosity increased as his friend's behavior and secrecy concerning the mine became more assertive.

It was on the third night of his visit that John became aware of Ralph's nightly activity in the mine shaft when, awakened by the noise and eerie glow, he attempted to follow it to its source. He met Ralph coming from the elevator. When he was questioned, an argument ensued, and John was ordered to leave the property at daybreak.

John had rented a room in the resort town. His lawyer's inquisitiveness was now piqued, combined with concern over his friend's bizarre behavior. He was determined to get to the bottom of this. Going north was now out of the question.

His inquiries among the locals in town brought him no nearer to a solution. While walking the beach deep in thought last night, he was attacked by an unknown assailant.

BOOM! The abrupt jarring of the elevator cage as it came to a halt at the bottom of the shaft shook John from his reverie.

With eyes acclimated to the darkness, he stared through the haze in the horizontal tunnel to small black forms suspended over a bubbling pool of viscous blue mud. Still fully creeping forward, he stifled a silent scream as the bloated and barely recognizable face of Ralph Rutherford came into view. His head was protruding from an immense hexagonal cell of drying mud being shaped by dozens of enormous and lethally venomous subterranean hornets. In the buzzing frenzy of their activity, John was undetected. Retracing his steps, he gained access to the elevator car and began his ascent.

Once on the surface, he frantically searched the explosives shed. With shaking hands, he managed to light the long cordite fuse and drop the taped bundle down the shaft.

He had just reached his car when the low rumble momentarily shook the earth and assured him of an end to this nightmare.

John Jacobs awoke with a sense of urgency. The cold spray from the showerhead reminded him that once again, the hot water had run out. *I must stop keeping such late hours*, he reminded himself. *This falling asleep in the shower has got to stop.* He laughed as the warm Arizona sunshine filtered through the bathroom window.

BINDI

2006

RIP, Steve "Crocodile Hunter" Irwin
1962–2006

Bindi felt the first pangs of uneasiness inch their path through her body that morning as the sun's rays started their ascent in the early-morning Australian sky. By midmorning, the feeling of melancholy and apprehension had completely enveloped her.

Twisting uneasily, she slid from her resting place atop the gentle island knoll into the placid lagoon waters. The instinctive undulation of her powerful tail propelled her huge body shoreward.

Upon gaining foothold, she ambled to the enclosure gate. It was here.

She was sure of the source. The confirmation of her perceptions was realized. The words overwhelmed her, rocking her being. The normally jovial assistant keeper of reptiles was in deep conversation with the zoo's veterinarian. 'STEVE IRWIN WAS DEAD!" Ambassador of conservation, wildlife warrior, crocodile hunter—whatever you may choose to call him—was gone. A great light on the world stage had been extinguished. His boundless passion for life and love of nature that had endeared him to so many had passed on as well. Our hero was lost at a time in this world that finds its heroes almost a species extinct.

POSTSCRIPT: Bindi, a female crocodile, was the oldest and the favorite resident of Steve Irwin's Australia Zoo in Queensland. Steve and wife, Terri, gave this name to their firstborn, a daughter, Bindi Sue Irwin, in 1998.

DUST TO DUST

September 28, 2006

He listened absently to the rhythmic click-clack of railcars rolling in cadence to the passing countryside as the sun highlighted the brilliant yellows and reds of the autumn leaves visible through the window.

His thoughts returned to that day much like this one when, as a young man, he had ventured on that memorable occasion so many years ago. Filled with the impulsiveness of youth, he had eagerly accepted the challenges life presented. As the conductor's voice trumpeted his destination's arrival, a slight smile etched itself across the time-worn face. It was all coming back clearly now.

It was as if yesterday had revisited itself. He made his way from the depot through streets now barely recognizable with development through the years. As he rounded the corner at Third Street and Fairfax Road, there stood the park, as if frozen in time. The ornate iron fence with park benches still encompassed that majestic oak tree as if invulnerable to the passage of time.

As he slowly eased his lanky frame onto the nearest bench, the words spoken long ago once more resonated through his memory. "There's nothing to it, kid. It's as easy as a bird's nest on the ground. All you have to do is…" Decades ago, the newspapers had bannered that robbery. Caught, convicted, and sentenced, he had endured the consequences of his decision that day. Thirty-eight years in prison, with marriage, career, and children-to-be lost to his culpable actions that day. Gone, too, were the two older accomplices and instigators to his crime, buried in numbered graves within the prison walls.

Evening shadows were lengthening as he cautiously made his way over the fence to that towering oak anchored on the knoll in the now-deserted park. His hands searched with deliberate determination the hollow cavity hidden in the upper reaches of the left fork in the massive trunk. His probing fingers felt then grasped the stiff leather of the weathered brown pouch.

He felt as though his heart beating could be heard as he alertly walked the distance back to his motel room, with discipline of incarceration stifling his urge to run through the darkness. Securing at last the door of his room, he placed the object of his quest on the nightstand. His shaking hands unwound the deteriorating drawstrings of the pouch. In the shrouded, incandescent glow, his eyes focused on the mass of debris now revealed.

This worthless vestige of molded residue had once been almost three-quarters of a million dollars in currency taken in that much-heralded bank robbery so many years before.

Vivacious moths circled the solitary lightbulb hanging in anonymity from its embryonic ceiling cord. The muffled sound of dragging footsteps could be heard through the open doorway as they made their way in slow retreat down the empty hallway.

MAGIC CARPET EXPRESS: AN AD LIB FOR MR. PETER PANSE

2006

The magic carpet express, he jokingly thought, could best describe his present mode of transportation as he prepared to depart for the journey to the ancient ruins above the jagged rock-faced escarpment in search of answers to questions left centuries before when the cliff-dwellers suddenly disappeared.

The intense dry heat of the Great Basin Desert was being cooled slightly by the afternoon's predictable breeze as he planned his ascent accordingly. The burro stood in steadfast readiness as he cinched the saddle to blanket. With practiced precision, he mounted and began the trek up the winding trail to the site of the ancient ones.

As he swayed gently to the burro's slow but surefooted gait, his mind began to wander through mists of time when this plateau was a viable and flourishing community for the Anasazi tribe of Mesa Verde. What was it that caused them to leave their elaborate city in the cliffs? The alarming bray of the burro shook him from his lethargy. He looked ahead just in time to see the diamond-backed rattler uncoil in its accurate strike to the burro's right foreleg. Before he could react, he felt the burro's stumbling pitch from the narrow trail. The accelerating plunge through the rushing air, mixed with the burro's terrified screams, left little time but for just one thought before impact. *Now at least I can end this writing assignment of Mr. Panse's before more pen is put to paper!*

NOTE: Mr. Peter Panse was a terrific teacher. I met him in 2006 at the Douglasville Georgia Senior Center. He was retired and had taught journalism in the New York City school system for over forty years.

He reminded me of another man and author, Frank McCourt, who wrote the trilogy of his life, starting with Angela's Ashes, in 1996.

THE COREY CAPER MYSTERY

October 5, 2006

Corey Caterpillar was missing! His absence was first reported to the police by Armando Armadillo when Corey stopped showing up at the Catalpa Tree Restaurant, where he had dined daily throughout the spring months.

Armando, the proprietor of the eating establishment, spoke with detective Wendy Wasp and her assistant, Darcy Dragonfly, concerning the disappearance of the local caterpillar celebrity.

"So," said Detective Wasp to the rotund owner, "Thursday evening three weeks ago was the last time you saw him?"

"Yes," said the amicable armadillo, "and knowing he had dined here exclusively since hatching, I am very concerned by this turn of events."

"Do you suspect foul play?" intoned the wasp.

"Not really," declared Armando. "Corey was well liked by all our patrons. He had grown quite large and fat while dining here. With his cheery disposition and talent for dancing, I doubt anyone would do him harm except his natural enemy, Robin Robin."

"What's that you say?" retorted Detective Wasp. "You suspect Robin Robin might be responsible for the caterpillar's disappearance?"

"Now, I didn't say that! Please don't go putting words in my mouth!" replied Armando irritably.

"Well, what do you suppose happened to him?" intruded Darcy Dragonfly suddenly.

"To tell you the truth, Corey was acting strangely that last day he was here."

"How so?" buzzed the detectives in unison.

"Well, that last day he ate very little of his favorite leaf meals and complained of being very tired and feeling strange before he left."

Unable to elicit any additional facts from the scaly restaurateur, the detective duo flew off to confront the person last known to have seen Corey Caterpillar since his disappearance, his natural predator, Robin Robin.

"Okay, Robin, you know why we're here. Start singing."

"Does it have anything to do with that green worm?" chirped the red-breasted robin.

"Now that's what I call a good guess, Robby old boy. Come on now, come clean! We know you have a feather in this caper!"

"Yeah, yeah. All you coppers think you have it figured out, don't you?"

"So you're denying any involvement?" buzzed the wasp.

"I sure am! The missus and I had four beaks to feed this spring. Earthworms, grasshoppers, bugs of all sizes, but a nasty-tasting green tomato worm like Corey? Never! The last time I saw that fat slug was over there!" Robin indicated the upper fork of a nearby mulberry bush.

The dragonfly and the wasp arrived at the indicated site within minutes and stared in amused surprise at the sight awaiting them.

"Well, this is not something we're going to be mentioning at headquarters," lamented Darcy Dragonfly as his large faceted eyes stared in the direction of the newly opened cocoon.

ANONYMOUS LADY

2005

Anonymous lady:

I had been planning to write you at some future date, when the time and my mood were right. I wanted to collect my thoughts about my birth mother and life before putting pen to paper. Most important is truth and not to paint a picture in words with anything other than the facts as I remember or perceive them to be.

Yesterday I received your card and letter. Today I opened and read them. The sincerity of your conviction to Christ is most evident in your words. But even more remarkable is the fact that you go beyond words and transform your faith in a higher power into actions among souls in crisis or despair, at crossroads of life, without direction or, as in my mother's case, nearing the end of life's journey with the sudden realization of "what you sow is what you will reap."

I want to take this time right now to offer my heartfelt gratitude to you being there to comfort her as the end grew near. While I chose not to fly from coast to coast, realizing the futility of it all, the time for reconciliation had come and past many years ago. Throughout my remaining days, I will always honor and hold in high esteem the compassion and empathy you gave to her in her last weeks.

I am not a vindictive person. Never at any time did I want my mother to suffer the agonies she endured hospitalized during the almost nine months preceding her death. But in my own defense, I can say it is hard to love someone who never loved you. No memories have I of an embrace or words to that effect can I ever remember. In my mind's eye, I was never seen as anything other than an obstacle curtailing, in some respects, her freedom to do as she chose. Her vassal and property under her complete control since she took possession of me at age seven abducted from my loving foster home. Fantasized did I of being kidnapped from royalty to servitude to do whatever she commanded whenever and wherever she saw fit to do so. Having a bad day? Bring me the whipping boy; he is here, and the one who sired him is not. So ashamed at gym classes that someone might question the bruises, welts, or even the few incidents that required ER suturing from "accidents" attributed to a young boy's activities. Thank goodness I grew up in an era when such things were never questioned and people never stuck their noses in the personal affairs of strangers.

So why didn't I go see her? That is a question I will continue to ask of myself, probably to my last day, though in truth, now I can see from my hilltop vantage the big picture, how the death of a young mother in a car crash at the age of twenty-three orphaned three little girls all under six years old. This tragedy, through the years, has affected four generations of people to this very day on one level or another. Had the road not been icy or the young French Canadian mother, Antoinette, from Nova Scotia, not had to work the night shift, I certainly would not be here typing this narrative. Left alone with an alcoholic father who basically abandoned them to church, neighbors, foster care, adoption, and very old paternal grandparents. Three little innocents left without a mother or a father, to survive as best as they could the conscious perceptions of this thing we call life. Put fifty yards behind the starting line before the race had even begun.

I inherited the futility of it all, a childhood of estrangement and verbally and physically abusive behavior whenever the mood arose. Some of it so horrible I do not want to remember, let alone ever reveal it! I was a constant reminder to the orphan girl herself of bad decisions, mistakes made, and innocence lost and robbed at the age of fifteen, perpetrated by a man in his early thirties. I am the result of a latex failure, she told me. This accident occurred on a blanket on the beach sands of Rocky Point, Long Island, New York, in July of 1946, adjacent to the immense rock that has stood at the surf line, forever bearing witness to the ebb and flow of mankind and their deeds, both good and bad.

In the time frame of the present day, I now look back at all the missed opportunities and questions whose answers are now eternally lost in the vastness of the universe, forever remaining unanswered. Opportunities to at least partially fit what few pieces of my puzzle have not been swept away like footprints in the sand, forever gone. Did I really exist, or will I awaken in some other life-form on a distant planet? All I ever wanted was to affirm that I did exist! My worst fear would be the answer no. I will now stop dredging up the mud; some things are better to be left buried, as you are well aware. Early on, I quit crying in my beer and moved on to the best of my abilities. I will, however, offer you a brief chronology of my life, if for no other reason than to repay you for the truth and candor, as evidenced in your testimony.

Carol, my mother, was born in Inwood, Long Island, New York, on December 27, 1930. Sometime in 1932, Saint Patrick's Day, I was once told, her mother, Antoinette, was killed in a car crash while driving alone. She was a married young lady in her early twenties and left three little girls behind. Virginia was five, Polly was three, and baby Carol was eighteen months old. Carol's birth date, I surmise, was probably the reason for being given that name, due to the proximity to Christmas Day. Antoinette's Christmas Carol, I would like to speculate.

These three little girls had the misfortune of having an irresponsible father. James, a heavy drinker known to be violent at times, abandoned his three little motherless girls in their hour of need to the winds and compassion of strangers and relatives. Often have I anguished over the total void of humanity exhibited by humans for their offspring, especially in times of crisis. Never in nature have I ever seen this anomaly manifested by creatures we call wild animals. Virginia was taken in by church folks and Polly fostered out to an affluent family. Baby Carol was taken in by her elderly paternal grandparents. By the time she was about thirteen or fourteen, her grandparents were dead, and she was basically on her own. Apparently, she met my sire, Charles, in a bar while still under legal age. She once mentioned the fact that her physical development began very early as a juvenile. He was thirty-two years old and she was sixteen when I was born on April 1, 1947. They had gotten married, but things did not work well, and she left him when I was about six months old. Apparently, one source of contention was how he still yearned for his first wife and son. Carol said I had a half-brother from that union. Of course I never met him. I was told by someone his name was Lee.

I was extremely fortunate and ended up being placed in a most wonderful foster care environment, with a devoted and loving older couple who had two other children in similar situations. My Aunt Betty and Uncle Roy were the warmest and most compassionate couple God had ever created on the face of this earth! They gave everything they had, materially and spiritually, to help children in need. I spent the next six-plus years in their nurturing care. I firmly believe, had it not been for the fact that I was blessed to be with them during my formative years, I would have never had the strength or will to survive in this life as I have. Aunt Betty raised me with all the love one could ever imagine. She taught us by setting an example every day, demonstrating her immense faith in God and her deepest love for the true innocents of this world found in little children or the mentally and physically challenged. By word and deed, she had taught me to love and care for all of God's creatures that fly the skies, walk and crawl the earth, or swim in its waters. Guardian angels, butterflies, and ladybugs—I learned my lessons well, and to this very day, they remind me of my sweet and dearest Aunt Betty. Once again, I repeat a fact indelibly stamped in my soul: I would never have survived this life without the time spent with Aunt Betty, my mother, my angel, my protector, and my teacher.

Our daughter Betsy was named in honor of my Aunt Betty, who passed away in 1967. I have always considered her my real mother. Her spirit remains with me always. She represents a perpetual shining light that could always guide me in my darkness, memories of a soothing voice spoken with wisdom and clarity, a reassuring hand on my shoulder in times of evil and peril. It is no small wonder that over a thousand people from the town of Farmingdale, Long Island, New York, showed up for her funeral, and each and every one of them knew her as Aunt Betty! I had arrived on emergency leave from Vietnam to be with my dying "mother" at her bedside, too late. I arrived just a few hours after she left this world. Uncle Roy said the last thing she said was "Tell Chucky goodbye."

I can still vividly remember our last time spent together. It was in May of 1965. I had gone to Long Island on my first annual military leave to visit and spend time with Aunt Betty and those I loved the most. When the day came to go back, Aunt Betty and Uncle Roy got dressed up to drive me to the airport. I still have the photo I took with them standing at the door of the back porch. In the fashion and protocol of their era and times, I see Uncle Roy with gray suit, white dress shirt, and a tie; Aunt Betty in her best coat, shoes, and matching hat atop her curly graying auburn hair, with that little gold cross she always wore on a golden chain around her neck. No smiles but eyes focused on me or the camera, with the sunshine prominently highlighting the features and contours on the right side of Aunt Betty's face. Uncle Roy is in the background shade of the top step. The hand and the glove, I think as I now look at the framed enlargement on my writing desk as I type these words. I have never liked goodbyes and have oftentimes gone to great lengths to avoid them. This day found me particularly soulful and quiet with memories of two little tow-haired boys and a slightly older brunette girl and also Billy, a mentally challenged man who used to run and play with us through this big old three-story house at the northwest corner of Staples and Secatogue Avenues. So many years ago, when youth was yet untainted and we lived in the time of here and now, with never a thought of tomorrow. We arrived at the airport, checked my seabag, and went to the boarding gate. Strangely silent, it appeared we three were deep in similar thoughts. Aunt Betty, with her gifted and intuitive maternal instinct, knew it too. I knew she realized that this was to be our earthly parting when, at the last possible moment, she ran out to me on that airport field, hugging me so tightly and crying so inconsolably before I boarded the plane that was to fly me off to war. If there be such a thing as heaven, past this great unknown, we will all be together again. If she is not in heaven, then no such place exists. I can feel that I am starting to dredge a little too deeply once again, and now is not the time to muddy these emotional waters.

Let me fast-forward this and just say that my life after Aunt Betty began in 1954 with Carol after being traumatically abducted while coming out from my elementary school class. Unexpectedly snatched up and flown down to Chesapeake, Virginia, from Farmingdale, Long Island, New York. To be *kidnapped* from the only home and love I had ever experienced was not pleasant, to say the least. My half-sister, Fay, had been born in 1952 from a different father, but they never married. We shared a bond, my sister and I. We survived the difficult years of constantly moving, changing schools, and seeing new men come in and out of our lives. We felt like the baggage, and they all knew we came along with the deal. Robert, another half-brother with different father, was born in 1959. I'm reminded of Carol's joke: "Just one to a customer."

Fast-forward. Cleveland, Ohio, April 1, 1964. Upon attaining my seventeenth year on planet Earth, my "sentence" was completed. I left immediately for the military boot camp, Hospital Corpsman School, amphibious training, a short seven-week tour of duty on a hospital ship at the naval station in Long Beach, California, and then on to Vietnam, starting in June of 1965.

I won't go into the details of ten years spent with Carol. She was a very troubled woman, as I look back. Alcohol, addiction to pre-scription drugs, polarized mood swings, a hair-trigger temper mixed with cruelty, emotional and physical, were the order of the day, as my sister, Fay, can attest to. Oh, we always had plenty of food to eat, a roof over our heads, and good clothes to wear. To all outward appearances, we were ordinary folks. But what went on behind closed doors and some that spilled out were a living hell. She hated us literally for being alive and never hesitated a minute to let us know it. She was a party girl, and we were the obligations in her path holding her back. Physical abuse (though not sexual) was routine, as were the ever-present vulgarities screamed at us almost daily. Her mental paranoia for control and cleanliness was driven to the extreme. If you have ever seen the movie *Mommy Dearest*, you can begin to understand. She hated me most, it seemed. I once overheard her saying to someone it was because I reminded her of my "sperm donator." The sins of the father visited on the son, I guess. I used to cry every night for years for my Aunt Betty, jamming the pillow in my mouth so as not to be heard. One time, I got caught, and she said the only way I would ever see my Aunt Betty again would be in a box. I vividly remember my sister's face being pushed into a plate of vomit after one of my mother's tirades had caused her to throw up at the dinner table. Even now, when I look back and try to bring up some happy moment of those years, I can't remember or visualize any. When I departed Cleveland, Ohio, in April of 1964 for the military, I never looked back. Getting away from all that was a profound relief. Regardless of what might lie in the road ahead, I felt as though I had just been released from a terrible prison. Shortly after that, she divorced Robert's father, whom she had married. Robert was then placed in a county foster home, denied by both father and mother. Sounds familiar? My sister, Fay, was sent to live with her father. Carol was now thirty-four years old and free to pursue life without children constraining her, and that she did with the gusto of a newly released prisoner, I am told. She was a very good-looking woman who could always turn men's heads and elicit wolf whistles while walking down the sidewalk. She parlayed this power and beauty into a lifetime of liaisons with rich, powerful, and influential men. She had a good life, being wined and dined and traveling the world with the best of those in the fast lane, believe me. To her vanity and credit, I'll always remember her as a good-looking woman for her age, and certainly not what she might have looked like in her last months, as described to me by my daughter, Betsy, when she visited her in the hospital. She was a strong woman, a survivor of breast cancer in latter years.

In March of 1968, after four years of service as a navy corpsman, serving one and a half tours in South Vietnam, I was honorably discharged. I went to Mexico to visit and then married my pen pal on May 31, 1968. Maria Teresa was a special young lady from Hermosillo, Sonora, Mexico. I had courted this beautiful young lady with thick brunette hair that came close to reaching her slender waist in the mandated traditional style her culture dictated, never going anywhere on a date without a brother, sister, or relative along as a chaperon. I laugh when I remember the times I spent on her family's living room couch with a Spanish-English dictionary in hand.

Today, forty-eight years later, we are still together and are learning more every day about real love, at least as much as I am capable of. We are survivors of the marriage wars. I have learned at long last to say the unspeakable, "I surrender," to the things I now know I am incapable of controlling. I guess this thing called love takes years, in my case, to mature and enrich, like the fine wine in a cask permeating its contents with love and respect that transcend the physical attributes, maturing like a rare wine. We had a lifetime of struggles. I came with a lot of baggage, some that will never be discarded. Ballast for when the time arrives to help dispense my ashes on that Rocky Point beach with the massive rock completing a circle that began this saga so long ago. I find that a fitting and balanced ending, like locking the door when you leave.

I, too, battled an alcohol addiction until 1990, when I grew sick and tired of being sick and tired. To stop drinking was the hardest thing I ever did. I am very proud to this day to say I remain clean and sober. The adventures and self-inflicted hardships upon myself and on my little family during my twenty-seven-year drinking career could provide voluminous material for another book, for sure, sadly enough. I will say that I was always a hardworking physical laborer, earning a top union hourly wage, who rarely, if ever, missed a day of work or, for that matter, ever took a vacation. This is for two reasons, the first being that in those days, there were always twenty guys hanging on the gate, ready to take your place. Secondly, my "drinking thinking" logic would never have allowed me to drink and "party hardy" if I failed not to work long and physical days in the pipeline fields. An interesting paradox, but certainly a true and vicious, never-ending circle of fact. But I was blessed to have chosen a special person to be my life mate. I really believe that the woman I married was chosen for me, as I met her shortly after attending Aunt Betty's funeral on emergency leave from Vietnam in 1967. If I could live a hundred years and love Maria Teresa more each day, I could never repay my debt to her. That includes her patience, tolerance, and forgiveness above and beyond the call of our marriage vows. We have two great children, Betsy and our son, Michael, who is happily married to a lovely lady named Lisa. Of course, our princess, Jessica, Betsy's daughter, born in 1998, our only grandchild and the light of our lives, completes my little family.

Carol, my mother, had visited on a few occasions while the kids were growing up and when I could send the airfare. The last time she was in my home was in 1988, when Betsy graduated from high school. I saw her once again in the summer of 2003, when I was attending a Vietnam reunion in North Carolina and drove down to Florida to see my sister, Fay, and visit Carol. I had hope at that time we could try to make new inroads on reconciliations, but I guess time did run out on us. God bless her, but she never really changed to become a kinder and gentler soul. She was hurtful to my wife. She always felt entitled, we being the planets that orbited and she the sun queen, having the world of planets revolve around her, or so it seemed to me. Everyone "owed" her something for her gracing them with her presence. Her wants and needs were always paramount to anyone else's. In her mind's eye, men were always "after something," no matter the occasion. She never worked after the age of twenty, to my knowledge; she never tried to forge lasting relationships that I am aware of, at least not within her immediate family. How do you love someone who never loved you? I did have the nurse hold the phone to her ear that last night. Possibly she could hear me over her labored breathing when all I could say was "God bless you. Go in peace, and I love you"? That was all I could say. I had no more words. I never wished for illness, calamity, or any hardships to befall her. I struggled with the cards I was dealt in this life, knowing there are no exchanges or throwbacks. To continue to "cry in your beer" or waste precious days of life feeling sorry for yourself is a despicable waste and is counterproductive, as I have learned. When you laugh, the whole world will laugh with you. When you cry, you cry alone. No one really cares. So reconcile with that fact and move on. Certainly, my sister, Fay, and brother, Robert, have their stories to tell. Despite all else, Carol was always out there somewhere on the horizon, lurking in the shadows, as I used to say. Now she's passed on, and if there be this place called heaven, I can see the little baby girl who never grew up running with outstretched arms to be with her mother, Antoinette, who had to leave her three little orphaned girls behind so many years ago.

Sorry to lay all this down. I didn't mean to write you a book, but there is so much more that went on. I have only scratched the surface of the tip of this mammoth iceberg. I will leave it like that. I just wanted you to know who was there for her on the final day to try to understand that there are two sides to every story. Now I have revealed the other side. They say you can never understand unless you have walked in their shoes. I say, no one can walk the halls of my thoughts or open the doors of my past unless I give them the key. I believe, if I were ever able to find the time and mood to write down all my life's story as I have experienced it through my perspective, all of it, from A to Z, I would probably find hard to believe. But it is my story, and I really did walk every step of that journey. I find some of it hard to believe, yet I lived it. How can I ever expect a stranger to feel the same?

That tragic accident of a young mother revealing yet another surprising facet of this saga. Antoinette was also an orphan, having lost both parents in her early teenaged years. My maternal grandmother died fourteen years before my conception. Poor Antoinette from Port Maitland, Nova Scotia, returning alone from night shift work on that snow-covered, icy road, the car sliding while trying to navigate a curve in the road and slamming into a nearby telephone pole, causing the bottom to shear in half and fall to crush almost every bone in the body of the twenty-three-year-old mother of three little girls whose only thought was of her little girls waiting at home for their mother's return. She was found the next morning exposed to the elements, according to the obituary I read from a local newspaper researched from that date. The article further stated that the top half of the pole was still suspended from the telephone wires on cross-beams strung from it, as if somehow an aerial cross symbol of the tragedy akin to Calvary. It marked the site where her bloodied and crushed body lay half-in and half-out from the open driver's side door. Her body was covered with a blanket of newly fallen snow, now asleep for the ages.

Many are the times I have pondered the fickleness of fate literally warranting cruel changes to the future of those three little innocents. A momentary flash in the darkness forever changing the course of destiny for those babies and the babies they will have and the babies of the babies. A cascading domino effect setting in motion a self-reinforcing cycle that future generations beyond these current three will be powerless to alter, be it for good or evil. A perpetual surface ripple on the pond of lives yet unborn.

When I decided to break my writing mold and venture from fiction, poetry, and philosophy to a biography of the reality of my personal experiences, I had no idea of the scope and intensity that decision would entail. All I can say at this point is, I will return to the less-intrusive and painless forms of painting pictures with words that I have enjoyed in years past, as described above. Thank you.

I have occasionally, at different times in my life, gone voluntarily to the edge and put myself in harm's way. The collateral effect of those experiences has had its rewards mixed also with anticipated repercussions. But the months it took me to uncover the remains of mental traumas long buried in my attempt to flesh out the bones or at least provide a basic framework of my private journey in this narrative shook me. The level of anxiety and mixed, heightened emotions, the starts and stops in the resurrection of this skeleton for a retrospective review of my iceberg, have surprised me. The vast remainder of the frozen behemoth shall remain untouched and go with my ashes when they return to the sea, where the genesis of all life began.

Maria Teresa and I have moved now to Georgia since my retirement in 2005. Betsy is now married to Don, and of course, our only grandchild, Jessica, an athletic young lady, now eighteen years old, lives within fifty miles of us. Michael and Lisa have moved to a new home in Apple Valley, California. He commutes down the Cajon Pass daily to Loma Linda University Hospital, where he is an administrator.

In conclusion, I will say to any that have read this to live for the moment as if each one will be the last, for there is no future in the past. Hone your senses with an edge so keen to cut through the fog that hides the Creator's beauty that surrounds us.

Charlie James Brown

POSTSCRIPT: As I just typed my name, I am reminded that Carol named me for the two male figures, her sire and mine, who are the two people in the whole world that could have given a damn less for me. Who said God doesn't have a sense of humor?

ABOUT THE AUTHOR

Charlie James Brown and Tom T. Cat

Charlie James Brown was born on April 1, 1947, and spent his childhood in Long Island, New York; Virginia; and then Ohio, where he joined the U.S. Navy (1964–1968). He graduated from Hospital Corps School and Naval Amphibious School. The author served briefly on a hospital ship before being transferred to an amphibious squadron, arriving in South Vietnam in August of 1965. He participated in Operation Starlite and seven amphibious coastal assaults in the First Corps area from Chu Lai north to the D.M.Z., assisting in casualty handling for the U.S.M.C.

Upon discharge in April of 1968, he stayed in Southern California and married his pen pal from another country that same year. His work career post military consisted of twenty-seven years in natural gas pipeline construction and ten years working for the desert city of Victorville, California, in public works as a sewer Vactor truck operator, then promoted to the Traffic Signals Department, operating an Altec double-bucket boom truck. At his retirement dinner in 2005, he quipped, "Having risen from the depths of the sewers to the heights of the signal poles, it is time to leave." That same year, they sold their desert home and property and moved to the beautiful state of Georgia to be closer to their only grandchild, now in her freshman year at Alabama State University in Tuscaloosa.

Forty-nine years of marriage later, they can look back with pride upon their daughter and son, both bilingual, college-educated, contributing members of society. Education was always instilled as a valuable tool in life to their children by both parents, neither having completed a formal high school education themselves, and they single-handedly raised their own little family with no outside help or advice.

The author is now seventy years old, and he remains very active by pursing his outdoor interests among the natural beauty and bounty of his adopted state and home. He can also experience the special moments, and sometimes hours, when the mood is right, and he can indulge in a lifelong passion, painting his pictures with words from an easel of his life's experiences.

CPSIA information can be obtained
at www.ICGtesting.com
Printed in the USA
LVOW08s1720040917
547295LV00003B/20/P